Cockleburr Quarters

Cockleburr Quarters

By Charlotte Baker

Illustrations by Robert Owens

PRENTICE-HALL, INC.
Englewood Cliffs, New Jersey

Cockleburr Quarters by Charlotte Baker
Copyright © 1972 by Charlotte Baker
Illustrations © 1972 by Prentice-Hall, Inc.
Printed in the United States of America • 2
Prentice-Hall International, Inc., London
Prentice-Hall of Australia, Pty. Ltd., North Sydney
Prentice-Hall of Canada, Ltd., Toronto
Prentice-Hall of India Private Ltd., New Delhi
Prentice-Hall of Japan, Inc., Tokyo

Library of Congress Cataloging in Publication Data
Baker, Charlotte, date.
    Cockleburr quarters.
    SUMMARY: A black boy grows as an individual
through his efforts to keep a half-blind mother dog
and her eight puppies alive.
    [1. Dogs—Stories]   I.   Title.
PZ7.B1696Co   [Fic]   78-37960
ISBN   0-13-139485-1

*This book is dedicated
to all Little Leaveners, of all
colors and ages, everywhere.*

CONTENTS

CONTENTS

I

THE PUPPIES

Dolph and two other boys were kicking cans one Sunday afternoon when they found the puppies under the Cockleburr Street Kingdom of Heaven Church. One of the cans had gone flying underneath the building, and being the youngest and the skinniest, Dolph was elected to go get it. He ootched along the sand on his elbows and knees. But even when his eyes got used to the darkness under the church, he couldn't find the can in all the scattered trash. He finally saw it and as he was reaching for it he heard the mewing of the puppies.

The sound came from a place under the middle of the building. "Archie! Perry!" Dolph called. "Looka what I found!"

Archie and Perry pushed their heads and shoulders under the building. "What? What you got?"

"Hush up and listen."

1

They all heard the puppies whimpering. They sounded like a nest full of baby birds.

"Puppies, I bet. Bet you they's a bunch. Come on!"

"Quit shoving!"

"I'm stuck." There was a sound of ripping jeans. "Ouch! I'm stuck on a nail."

Archie and Dolph lay helpless on their stomachs, shaking with laughter. Perry was fat, and Archie jeered, "You jeans stretched too tight on you to get caught!"

"I can't go frontways and I can't go backways," Perry wailed. "I'm stuck for good. Ouch!"

Dolph and Archie whooped. "You stuck forever. They gone have to tear down the church to get you out."

A man's loud voice interrupted. "Hey, you kids! Come out from under there!" He banged against the wall with a stick.

"In a minute," Archie called. "They's some puppies under here."

But the man went on banging and calling, "Don't you in-a-minute me. Git! Git out now and talk later."

"Uh-oh! It's Bruh Biggers," Dolph whispered. Brother Biggers was the preacher of the Cockleburr Street Kingdom of Heaven Church, and Dolph knew his voice well. He heard Brother Biggers preach twice a day on Sunday and every Wednesday night at Prayer Meeting. His voice was so loud it carried all over the neighborhood.

2

The boys began backing out, Archie and Dolph pulling Perry out between them. All the while Brother Biggers kept yelling, "Git!" and Perry kept yelling, "Ouch!"

"What you doing under there?" Brother Biggers demanded, when they stood before him. "Can't you see it's time for church? Everybody around here ain't heathens like your folks."

Dolph looked around and saw the well-dressed families driving up and parking their cars. He tried to brush himself off but Perry and Archie weren't about to stay for a lecture, Brother Biggers or no Brother Biggers. "Run," yelled Archie and the boys scattered. Dolph made a dash for his front porch across the street from the church.

Dolph's house was one of a group of rent houses all alike, known as Cockleburr Quarters. Each was one room wide and three rooms deep, with a porch in front and behind. They had been there a long time. If they had ever been painted, they weren't now. At one side of Dolph's house was the Alley, with more of the same kind of houses on each side.

There was just one thing that made Dolph's house different from the others in the Quarters. This was his mother's garden. Emeline Burch planted growing things wherever she lived. Out in back of the house she had made a real garden in a small space, with good sturdy corn and climbing beans and neatly staked tomatoes and sprawling squash. All around

4

the house she had planted things that smell sweet—
four-o'clocks and petunias and cape jessamines.

Dolph was bursting with his news about the puppies when he reached the porch. It being Sunday,
Emeline was at home and so was the rest of the family,
except James, the oldest boy, who was a soldier in
Viet Nam. Dolph stopped and thought for a moment.
His next oldest brother, Albert, was in the backyard
helping Emeline in the garden but Dolph didn't want
to go around there because he knew his mother would
put him to work. He hated hoeing and weeding.

So did Albert. Dolph could hear Emeline yelling at
him, "Pick it up. Pick up that hoe; we ain't anyways
near through."

"Aw, Mamma!" Albert complained.

"Not one child of mine willing to help grow the
food they puts in they mouth," Emeline said, "Only
James. Only James to help his Mamma, and him gone
away."

Emeline didn't talk much as a rule, but when it
came to James she couldn't say enough. Dolph felt
the same way about James. Wisht James was here, he
thought, I'd tell him about the puppies.

Dolph's older sisters, Clara and Janetta, were coming down the front steps, carrying their babies. Dolph
knew they weren't going to stop to listen to him. He
tried, anyway, "You know what?"

Clara smiled over baby Walter's head. "That's nice,
Dolph," she said. Clara liked to have everything nice.

5

Janetta didn't hear him at all. Some friends had driven up and she was calling to them, waving her baby's hand, "Harrison says, Hi! Hear? Say Hi, Harrison!"

The only ones left were Myrtis, his younger sister, and Uncle Leon. Uncle Leon was probably in the house taking a nap. That's what he was always doing, except when he was eating or smoking his big cigars. Dolph wouldn't have told him anything, anyway. He went over to Myrtis who was sitting on the edge of the porch swinging her legs. Myrtis was only eight, but she always listened to whatever he had to say. Since James left, she was the only person in the world he could depend on to do that.

Dolph sat down beside her and swung his legs while he told her about the puppies. "How many was they?" Myrtis wanted to know.

"I couldn't see. I told you it was dark under there. And Bruh Biggers was bugging us all the time to get out. Puffing out his chest and blasting our eardrums so people know he there."

"How you know they was puppies, if you couldn't see?"

"They was puppies. They was crying."

"Reckon where was they mammy?"

Dolph hadn't thought of that. But sure, the mammy dog must be near by. Maybe she was one of the dogs Emeline was always chasing out of her garden. There was no shortage of dogs or cats on Cockleburr Street. Most people owned some, or let strays stay around.

6

Emeline wouldn't, though. She made her children chase any dog or cat out of her yard. She said they were nasty.

"Let's go take a look!" Myrtis begged. She knew they couldn't go; Dolph didn't have to point out the cars and people coming to the Cockleburr Street Kingdom of Heaven Church. But she felt how excited Dolph was about the puppies. If they were special to Dolph, they were special to her, too.

"They sounded just like baby birds," Dolph told her. "I'd sure like to get a look at them. I'd like to see them first, before Archie and Perry."

They listened to the singing coming from the church. It was good singing; it made them feel good. They knew the tunes and could hear some of the words. The rest they made up to fit the sounds, so they could join in:

> Whaaat a friendly hammer cheees us
> Aaaall loud Simpsons greeeasy bear
> Whaaat a privy lid you caaarry
> Evvverything to garden prayer.

That one was slow and mournful and long-drawn-out. They liked it and sang every verse, thinking about the puppies in their nest in the sand under the floor under the feet of the people crowded into the church.

"Looka yonder!" cried Myrtis.

Dolph had already seen what she was pointing at. A dog was limping toward the church, carrying one hind

7

foot off the ground. She crouched, her tail tucked under her as if she were trying to make herself as small as possible. She was a black-and-tan, short-haired kind of a hound; sharp and bony on top but soft and sagging underneath. Her swollen breasts scraped the dirt as she crawled under the building.

"It's the mammy dog."

They would have run across the street after her, but with church still going on they just had to wait.

II

THE MAMMY DOG

Dolph never did get back across the street that Sunday
to see about the puppies. People were coming and going at the church long after dark. But the next morning he got up earlier than anyone else at his house.
He had put his jeans and sneakers right on the floor
by his cot and was ready to go.

Even so, Emeline caught him. "You eat a good
breakfast for a change," she said. "Want to be skinny
all your life?" They both laughed. Emeline herself was
skinny, and all her children looked like her: little and
skinny and black. "And don't you run off nowhere,"
she said. "You got to help with the laundry."

Emeline worked for the Caspers, a white family
who lived on the other side of town. She cleaned house
for them and cooked their midday meal. Since there
was no city bus service, Mr. Casper sent a taxi to pick
up Emeline every morning and take her home after
lunch. The Laundromat was right on the way, so on

9

Monday mornings Janetta went along to do the wash, and when Dolph and Myrtis weren't in school they went too, to carry it home in Dolph's old red wagon.

"Janetta! Janetta! Come on with that laundry!" Emeline shrilled.

The taxi driver was waiting, parked in front of the house, laughing at the ruckus. He had red hair and lots of freckles. People on Cockleburr Street called him Mr. Speck. "Hurry up," Emeline urged her family, "You can't expect Mr. Speck to wait all day, him giving you a free ride and all, sticking out his neck to help us."

"I ain't worried," Mr. Speck said. "When my boss finds out will be time enough to worry."

Emeline pulled Janetta into the car beside her. Myrtis slipped in after them, all three almost buried under the bundle of clothes. Dolph rode triumphantly in the front seat. He didn't miss a move Mr. Speck made, driving. Dolph was sure he himself could get in a car and drive it right off, if only his legs would reach the brake and accelerator. The taxi ride didn't last long enough to suit Dolph.

At the Laundromat, Dolph and Myrtis left Janetta inside tending the washer and dryer, and went outside. They wrote their names in the dirt with a stick. It was fun to see D-O-L-P-H and M-Y-R-T-I-S written giant-sized, with great loops and curlicues. They tried to imagine how big they would have to be if they really wrote like that.

When the washing was done and they were pulling the wagon-load of clean laundry toward home, Dolph

10

and Myrtis kept on playing the giant game. They looked down at the ants and other bugs they saw and felt enormously big and powerful. They pretended the bugs were people. "Got me a dozen!" Squush. "Got me a whole town!" Squush. "I squushed an army!"

Dolph dragged the wagon. Myrtis watched to see that no clothes fell off. Janetta followed slowly, leafing through a fashion magazine she had picked up in the Laundromat. Dolph said, "Play like we the bug-people instead of the giants. Play like they's great big people up there above us. Our trees is just like grass to them. Our houses is little bitty boxes—"

"Telephone poles is little bitty match sticks—"

"Streets is just ant tracks—"

Myrtis held her foot over an ant hill, ready to step. "If they wanted to, they could squush us with they great big feet." She looked up, then she looked down and carefully stepped to one side, where there weren't any bugs. "Great big feet."

"Great big feet!" echoed Dolph. "Great big feet. I hear them a-coming with they great . . . big . . . feet!" He looked over his shoulder. Myrtis joined in the chant. "Great big feet. Great big feet. I hear them coming after us with great . . . big . . . feet!" They began to run. The squeaky wagon bounced behind them and their hearts thudded.

Archie saw them coming when they were almost home. He ran to meet Dolph, and Myrtis dropped back without a word. She knew the boys didn't want

11

her. When she and Dolph were alone, neither of them thought about her being a girl and only eight years old. But it made a difference when Dolph's friends were around. Then, Dolph was a big boy and she was just a little sister, and they had nothing to say to each other. Dolph and Archie went ahead, one pulling and one pushing the wagon, making noises like jet planes taking off.

Janetta came next, taking her time and thinking her own thoughts. Janetta was fifteen. Ever since she quit school and had a baby, she had been living in a different world. She spent her time dressing and undressing Harrison, or washing and setting and spraying her hair. Somehow she and Dolph were always getting in each other's way these days. Even when she wasn't there, her cosmetics scented the whole house.

Myrtis came last, watching her small dusty feet to be sure she didn't step on any bug-people. But she kept an eye on Dolph and Archie to see where they were going. She was pretty sure they would go and look for the puppies under the church, and she was determined not to be left out.

The boys left the wagonload of laundry at the foot of the steps for somebody else to carry into the house. Then they ran across the street to the church, and Myrtis stayed just far enough behind them so they wouldn't notice her.

"I don't hear nothing," said Dolph, lying on his stomach underneath the church.

13

"Maybe they's asleep," said Archie, beside him.

"Maybe they's gone."

"Gone, hunh! Man, how's a little old rat-sized pup going anywhere?"

"Mammy dog could have carried them, that's how."

"They not gone. See right there?"

"Where?"

"Right in front of your face."

There was a dark shape in front of them, and from it came a low, menacing growl.

"That's her! That's the mammy dog—and she's warning us off!"

They waited, the boys and the dog, watching each other.

"No dog going to scare me," Archie said. The dog was silent, so he moved forward, holding out his hand.

The dog lowered her head and cautiously gave a long deep, rumbling growl ending in a sudden, sharp "Mmmwaaaf!"

Archie jerked back his hand and scrambled backward. Dolph followed. He was glad it was Archie and not he who led the retreat.

As they came out from under the building, there was Brother Biggers again, waiting for them. The boys were ready to run but the preacher surprised them. "You're just the boys I'm looking for," he announced. "I got a dime for every one of those puppies under there. I'll pay a dime a pup to the boy that brings them out."

A dime a pup. Archie and Dolph figured. There

14

ought to be at least five puppies, and there might be ten. They would make a quarter, maybe fifty cents apiece. But then, there was that mammy dog on guard.

"Well, what do you say?"

Archie said, "Dime won't pay me to get dog bit."

"What you talking about, dog bit? Blind, toothless puppies going to bite?"

"They mammy's under there with them. And she's got tushes like a big boar hog."

Dolph listened to Archie with admiration. He made them sound very brave to have gone so close to such a dangerous animal.

Brother Biggers seemed to think Archie was trying to get a better offer. "I'll pay a dollar for the lot," he said. "So, even if there's only one or two pups, there's a dollar for getting them out. How's that?"

"Right," grinned Archie. "As long as we don't have to go after them until that mammy dog's out of the way. I been as close to her tushes as I'm gone get."

Brother Biggers hesitated. "Oh, well," he agreed at last, "she'll have to come out directly and then you can get a chance to take the pups. Just don't be all week about it. I want them out of the way before Prayer Meeting night."

When Brother Biggers left, Archie strutted around bragging how if it hadn't been for him they wouldn't have been paid so much. They talked about what they would do with the dollar when they got it. It was almost as good as spending the money. After a while, though, they got tired of waiting for the dog to come out. Archie told Dolph to watch for her, and whenever he saw her out in the open to let him know. "Don't you go get those pups without me, man!" he threatened, leaning over Dolph to show how much bigger he was. "If you do, I'll whup you!"

That made Dolph mad. "I will if I want!" He yelled into Archie's face, and ran for home.

III

WHAT DOLPH OVERHEARD

Late that afternoon, Dolph saw the mammy dog come out. First she poked her head out and turned it way around to make sure no one was near. Then she dragged her body out and crouched against the wall of the building, listening. One of her ears stood up and the other hung down. At last she limped away with her tail held close.

As soon as she was out of sight Dolph was under the church wriggling toward the puppies, guided by their whimpering. There they were, in a shallow hole in the sand, but it was too dark to see how many. He put his hand in among them. They were warm and soft and throbbing. He could feel tiny paws pushing at his hand, tiny moist mouths and noses nuzzling at his fingers. They felt so funny and so good! A shiver ran from Dolph's hand right through his body. He lay there making silly puppy-noises, forgetting what he had come to do.

17

Then he remembered. "Hoo, man," he whispered, "How'm I going to get you out of here? You so soft and squirmy." He counted them as well as he could. There were eight or nine of them. It would take forever, crawling like a worm the way he had to, to carry them out one by one. If only he had thought to bring a box!

In the trash around him he found a big, empty paper sack which had once held cement mix. Placing the puppies in a huddle on the sack, he pulled it carefully after him as he backed out.

He could get a good look at them, now. They were rat-sized, sure enough, and toothless and blind. They were all colors: black, white, tan, black-and-white, black-and-white-and-tan, white-and-tan—and one was spotted like a leopard dog. Eight in all. They squirmed and mewed and rolled over on their backs and tried to roll back on their stomachs, waving their feeble little paws.

They want they mammy, Dolph thought. He felt mean, but he didn't stop to think why. He had to go to Brother Biggers and get that dollar. No, he didn't intend to keep the whole dollar for himself. But he was going to have the fun of bragging about it to Archie. It wasn't often Dolph had such a chance to be top man.

He left the puppies on the sack under a bush beside the church, and ran to Brother Bigger's house. It was just behind the church, facing another street. The preacher was at his supper table. He grumbled at being disturbed, and made Dolph wait while he swallowed the last of his pie. His wife got out a plastic laundry basket and a flashlight, and finally Brother Biggers pushed back his chair and started out.

It was nearly dark when they got to the place where Dolph had left the puppies. The sack was still there, but the puppies weren't.

"They were there, Bruh Biggers, honest!" cried Dolph. "They was eight of them. Somebody stole them."

"Nobody's going to steal puppies," Brother Biggers snorted.

Sister Biggers put her hand on Dolph's shoulder. "We believe you, Dolphie. But where have they gone?"

Dolph was wondering about Archie. He might have taken the pups, just to show he was top man.

"You know what I think?" Sister Biggers shook his shoulder to get his attention. "I think that mammy dog took them away."

"Eight of them?" her husband protested.

"She could of. Listen; don't I hear something under the church? Like before?"

Brother Biggers squatted down and tried to look under the building, but he was too stiff. He handed the flashlight to Dolph. "Here, take a look."

Dolph flattened out and turned the beam of light on the place where he had found the pups. There she was, the mammy dog, one eye glaring like a small red mirror. She was huddled around her puppies in their sandy

19

nest. She stared into the light, rumbling her deep, menacing growl.

Dolph backed out. "She's there, all right. Puppies, too."

"You see? If you'd just brought them with you to the house instead of leaving them here—! Now we got it all to do over again." Brother Biggers scowled.

"Never mind," Sister Biggers said with a nervous little laugh. "Dolphie will just have to earn his money, that's all." She turned to Dolph. "I expect the mammy dog is settled in for the night. But early in the morning, that's when she'll be on the prowl. You get the pups out early in the morning, Dolphie."

"Yes'm," said Dolph. He hated to be called Dolphie.

"This time, you put them in a box," Brother Biggers grumbled.

"And bring them to the kitchen door," Sister Biggers added. "There might be a piece of dewberry pie left for you."

Dolph thought the pie would taste better right now.

Brother Biggers started home. He stumbled. "Come on with that light!" His wife followed. Dolph heard the preacher say, in what for him was a low tone, "If he brings the pups in the morning, I can get rid of them on the way to Hillview. I go right by that dump on the old road."

Sister Biggers' softer voice said, "We don't get shut of them soon, we have a church full of fleas."

"You can't count on these kids, though. . . ."

Dolph hadn't stopped to wonder why Brother Biggers wanted the puppies. It made sense that they couldn't stay under the church forever, but he had just taken it for granted that the preacher would see to it that they were cared for. What he overheard Brother Biggers say gave him a shock. The preacher didn't want the puppies at all. He just wanted to get rid of them; and he was going to carry them off to a dump. He was going to leave those little, helpless, rat-sized, blind and toothless pups to die.

A part of Dolph that had been asleep woke up. Now he remembered things that had happened when he was too little to understand what they meant. People carried off kittens and puppies they didn't want. They told the children that somebody would find the puppies and take them home. Suddenly Dolph didn't believe that. He felt sick.

He knelt by the church and listened for the puppies, but all he could hear was the noise of the televisions in Cockleburr Quarters and the radio at the Corner Store and the children who were still playing in the Alley. Dolph saw Myrtis come out of the store, carrying a loaf of bread. He jumped up and ran panting to meet her.

Myrtis listened big-eyed to what the Biggerses planned to do with the puppies. It took a long moment for the truth to sink in. So this was what it meant when grown people took puppies and kittens away. This was what had to be. Because what grown folks said and did had to be.

Dolph tried to put into words how cute those

21

puppies were. "They looked just like a mess of speckled butter beans," Dolph said. He couldn't describe just how he felt when they hunted for his fingers with their little, wet mouths. But Myrtis understood. As they talked something took shape in their minds—a resolve that Brother Biggers mustn't ever get his hands on those pups.

"What you going to do, Dolph?"

Do? Dolph looked at Myrtis. He was going to have to do something; Myrtis expected him to. "I betcha I could make friends with that mammy dog," he said. "I could feed her and she'd get used to me. Then we could take her and the puppies somewhere safe."

"What you going to feed her, Dolph?"

Hoo, man! Dolph was stumped. "I don't know."

"Scraps?"

"What scraps?" There wasn't ever much of anything to eat left over at their house.

IV

THE LITTLE LEAVENERS

Early next morning, Dolph was up and watching when the mammy dog slipped out from under the church. He followed her, dodging in and out of the neighbors' backyards, careful to keep out of the way of anyone who might ask questions. That meant Archie, Perry and Brother Biggers.

The dog nosed around the garbage cans. Whenever she found a scrap of food she snatched it and carried it off to eat it in hiding. She didn't find much but egg-shells and potato peelings and greasy paper wraps, but she ate them all and she kept a good distance between herself and Dolph. Her ears were always twitching and her head was always turning to watch him. The way she turned her head so far around seemed strange to Dolph, until he realized that her left eye was blind.

Dolph and the dog were in Mrs. Randall's back-yard when Mrs. Randall came out to shake her mop. She lived in a house of her own next door to the

23

Quarters. She was a widow, old and overweight and crippled with arthritis; but she did her own housework, always wearing a fresh, pink dress. Her yard was always green and neatly cut. On her front porch there were hanging baskets of ferns, and on each side of her front walk was a long bed of violets and pansies. The Cockleburr Quarters children thought she must be rich.

Mrs. Randall saw Dolph before he saw her, so he had no chance to avoid her. "Now, which one are you?" She demanded. "You're one of Emeline's, but I forget which."

"I'm Dolph."

"Well, Dolph, you're up with the chickens this morning."

"Yes'm."

"Looking for something?" There were sharp eyes behind the old woman's spectacles.

Dolph shook his head, "No'm." But while he stood there the mammy dog was slipping out of sight.

"Well, then, how about running an errand for me?" Mrs. Randall beckoned him closer. "I'm going to fix refreshments for the Little Leaveners' meeting this afternoon, and I just discovered that I'm out of cake mix and low on coffee. If you'd go to the Corner Store for me I'd be much obliged."

Dolph hesitated. "O.K., but I got to do something else first."

"I'll give you a quarter to go right now."

Dolph grinned. That was different. He went into

24

the kitchen with Mrs. Randall while she wrote out a
grocery list. She kept thinking of more things she
needed. "I don't know if you can tote all this," she
said finally, looking at him over the top of her
spectacles.

"I can get my wagon," Dolph offered.

"That's the boy." She nodded. "And for a load like
this, I'll pay more."

Hoo, man! Dolph's eyes shone. Money for the
mammy dog!

Mrs. Randall smiled, "And what you going to spend
your money on, Dolph?"

"Dog food!" Dolph told her before he remembered
not to. The moment it was out, he wished he could
take it back.

"Dog food! What you want with dog food, Dolph
Burch?

If only he had kept his big mouth shut. Dolph said
nothing.

"With all the children your mamma got to feed,
you spend money on dog food?"

Dolph wasn't going to look at her, and he wasn't
going to answer. The more you told grown folks, the
more they interfered.

"The Bible says it's wrong to take bread out of the
children's mouths and give it to the dogs," Mrs. Randall insisted. "Don't you know they's babies at your
house need milk?" Mrs. Randall thrust her face in
front of his, so he had to look at her. "Answer me,
Boy."

25

"That dog got babies to feed, too!" Dolph was scared to argue with Mrs. Randall, but being scared made him mad; and anger and fear together made him stubborn. He wanted to yell, Hush your Bible talk and just give me that list so I can earn my money! But he didn't. Maybe she wouldn't even let him go to the store for her, now.

Mrs. Randall had been looking him over thoughtfully. "What dog?" she demanded.

"Just a dog," Dolph said, but the old woman wouldn't take that kind of an answer.

"You mean that poor, crippled, half-blind, gotch-eared hound dog, been coming through my yard?"

Dolph stared in surprise. The way she said it showed that she had not only seen the mammy dog, she had *looked* at her. Maybe even thought about her some. He nodded.

"And she's got puppies somewhere?"

Dolph nodded again. He watched her wrinkled old face. Something he saw there made him hopeful. She was thinking about the dogs, really thinking.

Mrs. Randall kept on with her questions, and finally Dolph told her about the puppies being under the church, and about Brother Biggers wanting them out. He told her that he was going to feed the mammy dog and make friends with her, so he could get them. He told her everything except that he wasn't going to let Brother Biggers have those pups. He didn't tell her that.

One thing about Mrs. Randall, she could listen as

26

well as ask questions. She sat quietly rocking, her gnarled fingers tapping an old Bible lying beside her on the kitchen table. When he was through, she drew it toward her as if she had made a decision. "Seems like there's more to that story," she murmured, thumbing through the pages. "About it being wrong to give children's bread to the dogs . . . Yes, here it is. When Jesus says that about the dogs, the people say, 'Yea, Lord, yet even the puppies eat the crumbs from their master's table.'" She looked at Dolph over her glasses. "Now, ain't that something, how the Good Book always has the answer? It's the living truth, the Book has got the answer."

She pushed herself up out of the chair and offered Dolph the grocery list; but she kept hold of it until she had finished what she had to say: "You run errands for me, Dolph, and I'll pay you what it's worth. But you promise me on the Book that you'll give your earnings to your mamma. Then I'll give you all my table scraps and kitchen leavings, and I'll get the Little Leaveners to do the same. And the butcher at the supermarket, I'll make a deal with him for you to pick up bones every week. All right?"

"Right!" Dolph's eyes were big and shining. Hoo, man! This morning when he woke up he'd had a big weight on him. Now it was gone. He felt light and bouncy, like a rubber ball. Scraps for the mammy dog, and money for Emeline. Wasn't she going to be surprised when he told her he was earning money! Dolph bounced off with the grocery list to get his old wagon.

27

As for the scraps, Mrs. Randall told him to come back that night. There was always plenty of leavings after a Little Leaveners' meeting.

Dolph got there after the meeting was over, but some of the Leaveners were still there helping with the dishes. Dolph had been wondering what in the world Little Leaveners were. It turned out that they were just women—some tall, some short, some old, some young, but mostly old. Mrs. Randall made Dolph come in and meet them. She told him their names and where they lived, so he could go collect the leftovers they promised to save for him. They didn't promise to have much, though.

"Dogs!" said Mrs. Whitaker. She was tall and light-colored. "If you want dogs I got four puppies to get rid of, and my daughter-in-law's got ten. Don't say dogs to me."

"Well, as long as I got a crumb, you welcome to it," Mrs. Collier said. She was plump and wore a tight green dress. "But crumbs is all you'll find at my house."

Mrs. Randall polished a dish with a fresh towel. "If we had a lot to give, we wouldn't be Little Leaveners," she said. "The lump—that's the world and all its wickedness—it's mighty big; and the leaven—that's us, with all our sins and weaknesses—it's mighty small. But the Book says, 'A little leaven leaveneth the whole lump.'" She looked down at Dolph, who was waiting as patiently as he could. It seemed to him that he was always waiting for grown folks to do what they

28

were going to do. Didn't they ever just up and do it, without talking it to death? He only half-heard and half-understood what Mrs. Randall said.

Mrs. Randall was the kind who never stopped until she said all she wanted to say. "Do you understand, Dolph?" He shook his head. "Speak up, Boy!"

"No'm," said Dolph.

"Well, this cake I made. See that?" There was a quarter of the cake left on the plate. It looked good. Coconut! Dolph's mouth watered. He nodded. "There's something in the mix that makes it rise. Just a pinch of white powder, but it makes the whole cake rise nice and light. Without it, you'd have a hard heavy lump—you wouldn't have a cake. Understand?"

Mrs. Collier laughed, her dress straining over her bulges. "You wasting your time, Annie Randall! That boy ain't taking in a thing you say."

"Don't be too sure of that," Mrs. Randall said. "A seed got to lay in the ground a while before it starts to sprout."

Mrs. Randall handed Dolph a big sack of leftovers. "Hold it in one arm," she told him. "You can carry the cake in the other hand." While she talked she deftly transferred the quarter of coconut cake from the platter to a paper plate and put it in Dolph's free hand, steered him to the door, opened it and pushed him out.

V

A LETTER FROM JAMES

Myrtis was waiting for Dolph. When she saw the cake her eyes grew bigger than they already were. "It's for us," Dolph told her. "And look what they give us for the mammy dog. Come on!"

There was a street light in front of the church, so Dolph and Myrtis didn't sit on the church steps to eat their cake. They went around the corner, on the side farthest from the Biggers' house where the shadow of the building hid them.

Myrtis said, "We could save some cake for Walter and Harrison."

"Cake ain't good for babies," said Dolph. "And coconut cake's the worst kind. The school nurse told us she knew a baby strangled hisself on coconut."

"Oh."

It didn't take long to eat the cake. They licked their fingers and lips, sticky with thick marshmallow icing and coconut. Dolph wondered where the little leaven

31

was in the cake. Just what were Mrs. Randall and her
friends talking about, anyway?

When they had finished they took the sack of scraps
and crawled under the church. Without a light they
couldn't see whether the mammy dog was there or not,
but when they tore the sack open and let the smell of
bacon rind and cornbread out, they thought they
heard a stirring.

They called softly, "Come on, Mammy, here's your
supper! Come on, Mammy, come to supper!" They
spread the sack open on the ground. The dog moved,
shook herself and they heard her ears slap. She didn't
come to them, though, and after a while they gave up
and backed out. The moment they stood up outside,
they heard the dog snatching and wolfing down the
food. They heard the puppies mewing because she had
left them. They heard sniffing and pawing as she made
sure there was no more to eat. And then the mewing
of the puppies stopped and they heard a soft thud and
a deep sigh as the mammy dog settled back into the
nest with her puppies safe against her. The children
smiled at each other in the dark. Their own stomachs
felt full and comfortable, and they knew that the
mammy dog felt the same way.

The door of their house opened and Clara called
out, "Myrtis! Dolph!" They weren't sure they wanted
to answer, until she called again, "Myrtis! Dolph! We
got a letter! A letter from James!" Then they went
running.

The whole family was gathered in the front room

listening to Clara read a letter from James in Viet Nam. Emeline had already read it, but she didn't care how many times she heard it. Whenever anyone came in who hadn't heard it, the letter was read out again. Eventually everyone in the neighborhood who had relatives in Viet Nam came by to hear James's letter and show off their own.

James didn't write about the fighting. He wrote about the interesting things he saw, like jungles and high mountains and twelve inches of rain in one day, and elephants and peculiar kinds of food and water buffalo. He wrote about the boys he met from all over the United States, and the things they told him. "Don't let anybody sell you that guff about moving north to one of those big cities," James wrote. "I seen some of those paradises before I left the States, and believe you me they make Cockleburr Quarters look like the Hilton. Guess what. I bought me a lot to build us a house on some day. That's what I think about when I get fed up with the Army. I'm paying on it each month. It's that lot third from the corner on the south side of Short Cockleburr Street, you know, right next to Mr. Holly. How about that? You all go look, decide what kind of a house you want, and that's the kind I'll build."

Short Cockleburr Street was only one block long. It was what was left of Cockleburr Street after it crossed Catalpa. It soon petered out into a dirt track which used to be an old road climbing Cockleburr Hill. The hill was steep and sandy and overgrown with

33

trees and bushes and briars. New streets had been built on top of the hill and on the other side, but there weren't any streets going straight up the hill.

"What's he want to buy a lot for? Man, with all that money he could buy wheels!" cried Albert.

Uncle Leon scoffed, "Take more than talk to build a house."

Emeline's eyes were bright. "James can build a house. He builds things in the Army; that's his job."

Janetta gave a sour laugh. "James get home, Cockleburr Quarters won't look so rosy."

Emeline snapped, "Shut your mouth!"

Walter bounced on the bed, gurgling. "He trying to say shut your mouth!" Myrtis cried.

Clara caught the baby up in her arms, telling him how smart he was. "Ain't he something else!"

"Harrison could say that three weeks ago," Janetta said, and Uncle Leon laughed as if she'd made a big joke.

Shut your mouth! Shut your mouth! Dolph yelled inside his head. He wanted quiet so he could think about James and his lot. Build a house? Who but James would think of something like that? Hoo, man! That James, he something else. Wisht he was here; I could ast him what to do with those pups. He went outside, slamming the screened door behind him.

34

VI

MAKING FRIENDS

Next day Dolph made the rounds of the Little Leaveners, running errands and collecting table scraps. He went by back ways to avoid Brother Biggers. He told Mytris to keep watch on the church while he was gone and report to him if anybody went near.

It seemed like forever to Myrtis until she saw Dolph coming back with his loaded wagon. She ran to tell him that Brother Biggers had gone into his office at the back of the church. As long as he was there he couldn't possibly see Dolph taking food to the dog. Dolph decided to risk it.

They crawled under and put the food about halfway between them and the nest. They could see the dog dimly, with her head up watching them and her lopsided ears listening to every word they spoke. They begged her to come and eat.

"She got to get used to us," Dolph said. "We come

35

twice a day with all this good-smelling stuff, and talk nice to her, she bound to make friends."

They tired of calling, "Here, Mammy! Here Mammy!" and started to think of names for the dog. They decided against Mammy and Gotch Ear. "I want to name her something pretty," Dolph explained. "A poor, old, crippled, blind, gotch-eared hound dog like her, I bet nobody ever called her a pretty name in her whole life."

"Gloria is a pretty name," Myrtis said softly. She had been saving that name for one of her own children some day. She thought it was so wonderful, she had kept it a secret. She had never even given it to a doll.

"Victoria is a pretty name. Gloria Victoria. Hoo, man! Now, that is a name!" Dolph said. "We can call her Vicky, or Tory. Or Glory-Tory."

They rolled the name around in their mouths and giggled. "Glory-Tory! Tory-Glory! Glory-Tory-Rory-Story-Dory-Bory-Lory—" They forgot to keep their voices low.

The dog left her nest. She wouldn't come to the food, but she came closer and crouched, waiting, a little way off. Dolph and Myrtis punched each other, whispering, "She gone make up! What'd I tell you?"

"Let's go away and let her eat."

"We'll come back tonight."

They backed out from under the church and stood up. There was Brother Biggers waiting for them with a rope.

36

They couldn't run anywhere he couldn't catch them, so they stayed where they were. Brother Biggers boomed, "She ain't let you git up close to her yet?"

"Nosir," Dolph answered cautiously. He couldn't believe it, but the preacher seemed to be in a good humor.

"I sure hoped to get them out sooner," Brother Biggers said. Dolph waited, wondering what was coming next. "Sis' Randall, she told me how you was going to feed the dog till she made up with you, so's you could get a holt of her. I guess that's as good a way as any. The Little Leaveners giving you scraps from their cooking, no dog is going to hold out very long, because they's champion cooks."

Hoo, man, Dolph thought. I should have rememberd that Miz Randall is in Bruh Biggers's church, and she was bound to tell him. But she's got on the good side of him somehow—guess it's her cooking.

Brother Biggers held out the rope. "Soon's you get close enough to that dog, slip a noose around her neck. Then we'll have her and her pups, too."

Dolph took the rope. He managed to say. "It's gone to take me a while. That dog mighty wary."

"Well, just remember, the sooner you get them out, the sooner you make the dollar."

Dolph nodded, and every morning and every night when he went to feed Tory he thought about what Brother Biggers had said about the Little Leaveners' cooking. Maybe it would work. Tory seemed more

friendly. She still wouldn't let Dolph touch her but every time he talked, she swept her tail gently across the sand.

Then came the night when Dolph slowly reached out his hand to Tory and she did not draw back.

Dolph put his hand on her head. She dropped her head on her paws, pressed her ears flat and let him stroke them. Her living warmth warmed Dolph's heart, filling him with a great, painful joy. Tory had made friends. Friends. But this feeling they shared was closer than friendship, closer even than family. Even with Myrtis, Dolph had to be on guard sometimes. People were always changing; they were never quite the same from day to day. But this stray, wary, mammy dog had given him her friendship, and she wasn't going to change.

There was no longer any fear between them. Outside in the world there was plenty to fear, but at least they could face that together. They lay together in the sand, their bodies throbbing in sympathy. Tory's flesh and bones were covered with coarse, dry hair; Dolph's were covered with smooth, sooty skin. At the moment that seemed to be the only difference.

Next morning Dolph brought the rope Brother Biggers had given him. It was time to go ahead with his plan to get Tory and the puppies to a secret refuge. He couldn't put it off any longer, or the preacher would lose patience and hire someone else to get the puppies out so he could take them to the dump.

Dolph untied the rope from around his waist and

39

showed it to Tory. He hated to do it. Somehow he felt in his bones that a rope was a fearsome thing to a dog like her. She had kept herself alive in an unfriendly world by keeping free of such ropes. He laid it on the ground beside Tory's food and let her sniff at it.

Tory accepted the rope because she accepted Dolph. The very next day she let him tie the rope around her neck. There was nothing to stop Dolph now from moving the dogs. His heart sank. Could he do what he planned, after all? It was easy to plan something, but different when it came to carrying it out.

Dolph watched the puppies trying to swim up out of the nest to reach their mammy. I could just take them to Brother Biggers like he wants, Dolph thought. That's what grown folks would say do. And why not? Weren't grown folks the ones to say? And Brother Biggers was a preacher; everybody listened to him. Yet Mrs. Randall, at least, had a mind of her own. She went to the Book, and thought about what she read there, and made up her own mind what to do. All that she had said about the lump of dough, and the little bit of leaven making it rise—Dolph still didn't know exactly what it meant, but Mrs. Randall made him feel like he could do things if he tried.

He rolled over on his back and lay quiet for a long time, trying to make up his mind. A draft moved under the church, cooling his hot skin. Tory slept beside him, and Dolph might have drowsed off, too, if he hadn't felt a little warm, wet nibble on his ankle. He lifted his head to look. One of the puppies was there, nuzzling

40

at his leg. There was another, blundering out of the nest. Dolph crawled closer and saw that several of the puppies had their eyes open. That settled it. If he didn't act at once, those puppies were going to be crawling right outside, and Brother Biggers was going to jump on them like a duck on a June bug.

Dolph dug the nest deeper, to keep the puppies in there a little longer while he made his preparations. He was resolved to carry out his plan. He crawled out from under the church, feeling a thousand years old.

When he got home he oiled the wheels of his wagon so they didn't squeak much. He filled two old syrup buckets with water and put them in the wagon, together with a sack of food scraps and a battered iron skillet without a handle, which would make a good drinking bowl. He covered the load with an empty grocery carton and set out up Short Cockleburr Street.

As he passed the vacant lot that belonged to James, Dolph thought about the new house James was going to build. There would be room enough for all of them then, even the dogs. Dolph could already see that house, as clearly as he saw the old wrecked car body someone had left on the lot. He felt lighter and younger and quicker and more sure of himself now, although that was where the steepest part of the hill began.

He pushed and tugged his wagon up Cockleburr Hill, stopping often to pull the burrs off his jeans. He had to break down some bushes and detour around briar patches before he got to where he was going.

41

It was a shack which hadn't been used for years. Two summers ago Dolph and his friends had played in it nearly every day, but they lost interest in it when the Parks Program was started. Dolph remembered it because he needed a place to hide Tory and her pups.

He pushed the sagging door open and hauled his load inside. He looked around the small front room. The door into the back room had been nailed shut. The roof was leaky. The glass was broken out of the windows and most of them were boarded up. Some of the floorboards were rotting. There was trash everywhere. It was a refuge for Tory, though. She wouldn't be choosy.

Dolph left his supplies, closed the door and hurried down the hill. The rest of the day he was so excited he couldn't speak.

VII

NIGHT FLIGHT

Dolph had to wait until dark. After dark he had to wait until bedtime. And as if that weren't enough, he then had to wait until Albert came home and went to sleep. Of course, Albert was late.

Dolph lay on his cot on the porch and dozed. Whenever he half-fell asleep, he would wake up scared that it was morning and he had lost his chance. Then he'd get up and look into the front room where Albert and Uncle Leon slept, and see Albert's side of the bed still empty, and crawl wearily back to his cot. Once he dreamed that Brother Biggers came up the steps, booming, "Where those puppies?" But he woke to see that it was Albert coming in at last. Dolph lay still. It wouldn't take Albert long to go to sleep.

Albert was snoring. Now was the time. But Dolph could still change his mind. He could lie right there in peace and comfort and nobody would blame him. Then he thought of Tory under the church, curled around her pups. He thought of the way she rested her heavy head in his hand and flattened down her ears to be rubbed. She counted on him and the food he brought. The pups depended on her; and she depended on Dolph.

Dolph got up and pulled on his jeans. He had left his wagon under the church, out of sight. He looked up and down the street. He could hear cars in the busier streets beyond, but nobody was stirring on Cockleburr Street. Like a moth he flitted across the lighted area and melted into the shadow at the side of the church.

Pushing the carton ahead of him, Dolph crawled under the building for the last time. Tory met him with an anxious whimper. She wasn't used to his coming so late. It was pitch dark where they were, but she knew who it was. She gave Dolph a big swipe with her tongue from his chin to his hair. He giggled and felt calmer. He had planned just what to do. Now he went ahead and did it.

It would have been easier with a light, of course, but Dolph managed without. Carefully he located the puppies by touch. He lifted them into the carton, counting so he'd be sure to get every one. Tory nuzzled each pup and nudged at his hands. She didn't like what was going on, but Dolph was her friend, and that was that. When he crawled out, she followed him and the box that held her precious puppies.

She would have followed anyway, anywhere, but Dolph put the rope around her neck to make sure. He

44

couldn't risk letting her out of his sight. She walked beside the wagon as he pulled it up the street. He had to walk on the sidewalk, right under the street lights, until he reached the last house on Short Cockleburr Street. Beyond that was the dark. Dolph couldn't wait until he covered the short distance along the lighted street. He thought everything would be all right after he reached the darkness. But when the light faded out behind him, he discovered that he was afraid—more afraid than he had ever been before in his life.

He had never been out by himself beyond the lights and houses in the middle of the night. It was almost as dark ahead as the black space under the church; and much, much bigger. There weren't even any stars. The track he thought he knew so well had simply vanished. Every step he took, he stumbled. Although the air was heavy and warm, the back of his neck felt cold. He stopped. He couldn't go on. His heart was thundering in his ears. In a minute he was going to hear the thudding of those great big feet. Great big feet. I hear them a-coming with they great . . . big . . . feet. And if he did, he was going to turn around and run like a rabbit.

There was a flicker of light in the sky, then a long, low rumble of thunder. Dolph nearly jumped out of his skin. Tory pressed, trembling, against him. Then the whole hillside in front of them was lit up. There was the white, sandy track; there were the briar patches; over there was the big catalpa tree. Across from it was the deserted shack.

The scene blacked out. Dolph stood, blinded. Tory

45

was pulling at the rope he held. He heard her sniffing at the ground. All the smells and sounds of the night meant something to Tory, and she could see better than he could in the dark, even with her one eye. She knew the old shack, having holed up under it often in the past. She feared the storm, and wanted shelter.

With Tory leading purposefully and lightning sometimes showing the way, they climbed on. The worst was almost over; all Dolph had to do was open the door of the shack and walk into that pitch-black room. But even that wasn't as bad as Dolph had dreaded. Enough light flickered through the open door and between the boards on the windows to show him all he needed to see. He took the puppies out of the box and placed them on a mass of old newspapers in the corner. They mewed for their mammy. Tory padded over to them and nudged them into a neat pile.

"Lie down, Tory," Dolph whispered. Nobody was going to hear him, but he whispered anyway. "Lie down. This is your bed. You'll be O.K. Look, your supper's all ready for you. And I'll be back tomorrow as soon as I can."

Tory sniffed around the room, found her food but didn't eat it; maybe she was too excited. She lapped up a lot of water. Dolph heard her. Hoo, man! He'd have to bring more water tomorrow.

The lightning came oftener and the thunder louder. A wind was rising. If he ran, Dolph thought, he might get home before the rain. He hated to leave Tory shut up. He told her so, and she panted into his ear, tickling him. He waited for a flash to show him the way, then he left the shack and closed the door behind him.

The rain was coming, all right. With the empty wagon bouncing behind him, Dolph ran down the hill. The wind pushed him from behind, and he felt as if he were flying. He couldn't keep it in. "I done it! I done it!" he yelled. In spite of everything, he had got Tory and her puppies away to a safe place. Brother Biggers wouldn't get his hands on them now!

He came down Cockleburr Hill bounding and sliding and running ahead of the storm. "Hoo, man! Hoo!" He yelled at the top of his voice. But nobody heard him for the thunder.

VIII

MADAM ASTRO

In the gray light of a rainy day, Dolph's situation looked doubtful. What would he tell Brother Biggers? What would he tell Mrs. Randall? He would have to stay out of their way for a day or two, but he couldn't do it forever. That would mean he couldn't run errands for the Little Leaveners; and that would mean he would get no food scraps. Then how would he feed Tory and the puppies?

Dolph's secret weighed on him, but he was determined to keep it. Now that he had Tory and the puppies all to himself, he wasn't about to let anybody interfere. He was the one who had made friends with Tory, and he was the one who had brought her and her family to safety. He was the one who had to feed them, wasn't he? It was nobody else's business.

Dolph dreamed up some lies he could tell the preacher if he had to. That the puppies died, or that someone else came along and took them. The problem

48

was, he'd have to tell the same lie to Mrs. Randall.
And lying to her wasn't easy, with her watching him
over her spectacles and tapping the Book. Things
did not look good until one afternoon when he met
Archie and Perry coming from the Corner Store. "Hey,
look!" Perry cried, waving a dirty pink card in Dolph's
face. "Guess what!"

"What?"

"Looka what it says on this card."

Dolph read:

SEE MADAM ASTRO
She's got blue gums and X-Ray eyes.
She locates lost articles, missing persons and buried
treasure.
No charge for a FREE reading.
Old Perkins farm near city limits on Oak Flat Road.

Archie said, "The man give me this, he said Madam
Astro knows where they's a pile of gold bricks buried
on the old Perkins farm."

"And you can dig all day for fifty cents."

"Haw! Haw! Haw!" scoffed Dolph.

"No kidding," Archie said, and Dolph saw he was
serious. "Man give me this card, he'd been over there
hisself, and they was more'n a dozen folks out there
digging. They had sacks and buckets!"

"How come him handing out cards, then, instead of
digging?" Dolph wanted to know.

"Madam Astro paid him to hand out cards, that's
why," Archie answered. "She paid him good. He said

he was going to go back and dig some, soon as he give out all the cards." He lowered his voice. "And he said she got blue gums, all right."

Dolph's eyes rounded. "I never see no blue gums."

"And X-ray eyes! She can look through walls and right down through the ground and see what's there," Perry said. "Why don't we go take a look, hunh?"

"It'd cost."

"No, it wouldn't. See, it says so right here: 'No charge for FREE reading.'"

"Reckon what does that mean?"

"It means she reads you with her X-ray eyes."

"We could go look." The old Perkins farm was less than a mile away. They could walk there and see what was going on, and stop on the way back at the swimming pool to cool off.

On their way they talked about fortune tellers and witches and spirits and people who found diamond rings in fish's stomachs and lost wills in mattresses and thousand-dollar bills up chimneys. Perry said his grandmother saw a ghost when she was a girl. It was the ghost of a man carrying his own head. He asked her to help him put it back on his neck. The boys thought that was hilarious.

As they came near the old Perkins farm, they saw a number of cars parked along the road in front of a small frame house. There was a crowd of people in the yard. Behind the house was an old barn and cow lot, surrounded by a tumbledown fence. That's where people were digging.

Dolph and his friends joined the crowd in front of

the house. They couldn't see what was happening up front, but a man standing on the porch was chanting like a carnival barker: ". . . right this way, folks. . . won't be long. . . step right up for your free reading! Madam Astro with the X-ray eyes. . . treasure in your future, treasure in the ground. Next! Don't shove, folks. Time for all. . . right this way!"

The people around them were both black and white; mostly men and boys, but some women as well. They all looked solemn and spoke in lowered voices, as if they were at a funeral. Now and then excited cries were raised back in the lot. When this happened, the crowd surrounding the boys would shift. Some would run off to see what was happening, while others would move up to take their places in line.

Before they realized it, Dolph, Archie and Perry were in the middle of the crowd and halfway to the house. They looked at each other, big-eyed. Shouldn't they shove their way out now? They hadn't really meant to let Madam Astro read them with her X-ray eyes. But they could feel the eagerness of the people around them, all expecting great things, and they began to expect great things, too. They let themselves move forward with the crowd.

At the foot of the steps they could see the man above them calling out, "Next! Six at a time, folks. Half-a-dozen at a time can go in for a free reading. Madam Astro can tell you if your luck is going to change. Madam Astro can see money in your future. With her X-ray eyes, Madam Astro can find gold wheresoever it may be hidden. No shoving, please!"

Money in your future! Hoo, man. The boys grinned.

They were on the porch. Next thing they knew, the door of the house was opened and they were pushed into the front room, together with two men and a woman. Although the shades were down and the light was dim, they could see the backs of the people who had gone in ahead of them leaving by another door. The air was hot and smelled of burning incense.

The only furniture in the room was a table and chair on a low platform against one wall. At the table sat a large, black woman dressed all in black. A light from a bowl on the table before her shone up into her face; but instead of showing what she looked like, it made deep, distorting shadows. Her eyes seemed to be closed. She sat very still. Suddenly, someone clapped his hands. Madam Astro bared her teeth—and sure enough, her gums were blue!

She raised her hands and pulled a long, black veil down over her head and shoulders. She spoke through the veil in a hoarse, muffled voice, "Stand in front of Madam Astro in a line. Madam Astro will read for each in turn. One fortune for each. Listen carefully as she speaks. Madam Astro does not repeat."

The woman in Dolph's group grabbed at the boys and pulled them into place on one side of her. Dolph found himself the first in line, with his heart pounding so he couldn't think, much less hear. His whole body was bathed in perspiration. He tried to listen, tried to understand the words that came muttering through the black veil.

The muttering stopped. Madam Astro pointed at Dolph with a fat finger, and said in a slow sing-song:

> "First Boy.
> Two, four, six, eight,
> Plus one. Your need is great.
> Add your age and start at the gate.
> Dig, Boy, Dig!"

The pointing finger moved and jabbed toward Archie.

> Second Boy.
> In the corner,
> Under the tree,
> You'll be lucky
> With number three."

It was Perry's turn. He was shaking and swaying. As the finger waved toward him, he sagged heavily against Archie and moaned.

"Git that boy out of here," the voice behind the veil ordered sharply. "He's going to pass out."

Dolph and Archie hurried to the back door with Perry stumbling between them. They got him outside somehow and put him on the back steps with his head between his knees. Pretty soon he could sit up and drink a glass of water somebody brought him. In a few more minutes, he jumped up and said he was going home.

"Let's watch them dig awhile, first," Archie said. But Perry wouldn't stay, and the others were afraid to let him go by himself, the way he looked. He wouldn't talk at all on the way home. He just rolled his eyes and mopped his dripping face. No, he didn't want to go swimming. He just wanted to go home.

When they got to Cockleburr Quarters, Perry kept going, but Archie stopped to tell Dolph, "She said I'd be lucky. All I'll need is a shovel, and I know where I can find one. They got every kind of a shovel they is over at the Project." A housing project was being built on the street behind the Quarters. They could see the brick apartment buildings above the plank fence along the property line at the end of the Alley. There were all sorts of interesting tools and materials there.

Archie went on. "I just got to wait a while, that's all, on account of the ball game. Coach'd skin me, man, if I missed that. I'll stop by for you day after tomorrow afternoon."

"I won't be home," said Dolph. He had been studying what Madam Astro had told him. It was scary, the way she knew about Tory and the pups. "Two, four, six, eight"—that was the puppies. "Plus one"—that was Tory. "Your need is great"—hoo, man, now how in the world did Madam Astro know that?

He was sure he had figured out what Madam Astro's reading meant. He wasn't going to wait until Archie was ready to go back and dig. No way! Dolph wasn't going to wait a minute longer than he could help.

IX

FOOLISHNESS

Before he could dig for the treasure, Dolph had to get fifty cents. The man said for fifty cents he could dig all day. But to earn it he had to ask Mrs. Randall for work. Could he do that without her finding out what he had done with Tory and the pups? She and the Little Leaveners were so thick with Brother Biggers, telling them anything was the same as telling the preacher.

Madam Astro's words went round and round in Dolph's head. He hadn't really believed in the gold bricks until she read out that verse. But if she knew about Tory and the eight pups and Dolph's great need, she must know about the buried treasure, too. And then, there were all those people. That many people couldn't be wrong, could they? The gold must be there, waiting to be dug up, and Madam Astro must have seen it with her X-ray eyes.

Dolph knocked at Mrs. Randall's back door. She invited him in, scolding him for staying away so long. How was she, an old, crippled-up widow woman, expected to get along without help from the young and spry? She had just about decided she would have to call Mr. Speck to take her to the supermarket.

"I brought my wagon," Dolph said. "I can go right now."

But Mrs. Randall made him sit down at the kitchen table and eat a peanut butter sandwich while she wrote out a list. Then she began to talk.

I should have known better than to come, Dolph thought as he waited for her to finish. She's like the rest. Worse. You ask grown folks to help you, they turn you inside out.

"I'd a thought you'd made friends with that mammy dog by now," Mrs. Randall said. "You must not be going about it the right way. Either that or she's an outlaw. Some dogs gone wild, ain't never going to civilize." She watched Dolph over her spectacles. "Dog won't civilize ends up being shot."

"Not Tory!" Dolph cried. "She's civilized."

"So you say."

"Well, she is."

"So you say."

"She is! She done made up with me."

"Then why is she still under the church?"

"She ain't. I got her out!"

Mrs. Randall smiled. "So that's why you haven't

been around here looking for work. Brother Biggers paid you the dollar for bringing him the puppies. Did he pay you anything for the mammy dog?"

Dolph looked away. "He don't know about it, yet."

"Don't know? How you going to get paid, then?"

Dolph felt about ready to explode. "I ain't going to tell him. I ain't going to tell him nothing about those pups. He wants to carry them off to the dump. If I give him Tory on a rope, he'll take her off, too. No way. Bruh Biggers don't get his hands on those dogs."

Now he'd said it. Dolph sat still, waiting for the roof to fall in. But Mrs. Randall didn't seem surprised. She sat calmly, nodding and rocking.

Whew! Dolph leaned back in his chair. Clear sailing now. He had told her. He'd told her and she hadn't said anything. No advice. No questions. So that's how people did it. They just said what they was gone do and nobody argued with them. Hoo, man!

"But how you going to feed those dogs, Dolph?"

"Same way I always feed 'em. Scraps."

"But when they get bigger, what then? You'll have to buy food."

Dolph burst out with his plans. He was going to dig at the old Perkins farm, dig up enough gold to feed those dogs for the rest of their lives. Mrs. Randall went off like a skyrocket.

She had already heard about Madam Astro, and was ready with a powerful sermon. First, she preached

58

about people trying to get something for nothing. She said if he didn't learn to put in a day's work for a day's pay he'd never amount to anything. She thumped the Book. "Like it says here, 'If any would not work, neither should he eat.' "

"Digging is work," Dolph stuck out his lower lip.

She stumped around the room. She raised her voice. She talked about wisdom and folly; how foolish children wouldn't listen to their elders, but thought they knew better. " 'Fools despise wisdom and instruction,' " she read out of the Book. " 'The way of a fool is right in his own eyes; but he that harkeneth to counsel is wise.' "

Hoo, man, thought Dolph. If I was wise I wouldn't be here. But where else could he go? Here in Mrs. Randall's neat kitchen he had found the help that had brought him and Tory this far. When he asked Mrs. Randall questions, he got answers—whether he liked them or not. He huddled in his chair, making himself as small a target as he could. Wisht she'd quit bugging me, he said to himself, but he knew better than to say it aloud. He twisted his legs around the chair rungs and held on.

Mrs. Randall was pushing the Book under his nose. "You listen to me, Dolph Burch. I been right here in this house almost as long as the Quarters been there. Me and my husband worked for the man that built those rent houses. He owned all this land and built us this house and give it to us 'cause we earned it. We sure enough earned it!

59

"And I can tell you that money don't grow on trees like persimmons; and it don't grow in the ground like turnips, neither. Ain't you got yourself into enough trouble taking on a mess of hungry dogs that ain't no good to nobody? That's foolishness, and I told you so to start with."

Dolph hated to be called foolish. It hurt. And it hurt to hear Mrs. Randall say that Tory and the pups were worthless. That hit a nerve somewhere inside him that twinged like a sore tooth. "If they no good, I'm no good," he muttered.

The old woman sat down and wiped her face with her apron. She took off her glasses and wiped them, too. She hadn't meant to call him a fool, Dolph could see that. He tried to explain. "I don't care if they no good to nobody, makes no difference. They looking for me to feed them. If I don't, nobody will."

"I know, Dolph," Mrs. Randall said gently. "Your foolishness is a merciful kind of foolishness."

Dolph's spirits rose. But Mrs. Randall wasn't through with him, yet. She was off again about Madam Astro. "But get-rich-quick, fortune-telling foolishness is sinful, and you better listen to me when I tell you so." She paused for breath, then tapped the Book for his attention. "Now, Dolph, I ain't going to turn my back on you in your folly, but you got to promise me two things."

"What?" Dolph asked cautiously. He wasn't going to promise to give up Tory and the puppies; and he wasn't going to promise not to dig for the treasure.

60

"You got to promise to keep on earning and giving what you earn to your mamma."

Dolph thought about that. He would do that, all right; but just this once he would ask Emeline to give him back fifty cents. "Right," he agreed.

"And you got to promise me not to tell no lies. That means, you got to tell Brother Biggers the truth about the puppies, if he asks you."

"I can't do that!"

"You tell him the truth," the old woman repeated firmly. "But you don't have to tell him nothing till he asks you." she smiled. "And you don't have to tell him *everything* you know." She put her hand on Dolph's shoulder to help her rise.

"Right!" Dolph grinned back at her.

At last she gave him the grocery list. By the time Dolph got back from the store, she had called the other Little Leaveners and arranged for more chores for him to do. Dolph was busy nearly all day, and earned a good amount.

Emeline was working in her garden when he went to give her the money. She was digging and weeding and staking tomatoes and beans. She would have put Dolph to work immediately, but when she counted the money he gave her she decided he'd been working hard enough for one day. She rubbed his head with her thin, calloused hand. "You're a good boy, Dolph."

Dolph agreed with her. He was proud of himself. Albert never had money to give his mother, he was always asking her for it, instead; and so were Janetta and Uncle Leon. It was James who saved money, and sent some home. Clara, too, had a steady job and paid for her keep. Dolph would rather be like James and Clara than like Albert and Janetta and Uncle Leon. It made him feel good to please his mother, as long as he didn't have to weed the garden.

"Here." Emeline gave him back two quarters. Dolph grinned. Fifty cents, and he didn't even have to ask for it! Tomorrow couldn't come soon enough for Dolph.

X

DIG, BOY, DIG!

Next morning Dolph was able to give Tory a big breakfast. The table scraps he collected were extra good; somebody had been cleaning out the refrigerator. There was a soupbone, besides. But no matter how much he brought her, Tory always wanted more. The puppies were hungry, too. They waddled along underneath their mother, hanging on to her breasts, whimpering when she shook them off.

All but the white one. He was still swimming instead of walking as the others did, and something was wrong with his eyes. He couldn't find his way back when he was pushed out of the heap. Dolph picked up the puny pup. He felt how light he was, and saw that his eyes were sticky and his nose ran. He looked sick, but Dolph didn't know what to do about it. He had heard that there was a runt in every litter. Maybe it had to be that way. He compared him to the other pups. "Even your fleas smaller than theirs," he murmured.

Dolph didn't spend much time with the dogs that morning. He was itching to start digging for the buried gold. It was a long way to pull the rickety little wagon, but he thought he'd better take it to haul home the treasure. Myrtis helped him load it with some empty cartons, an egg sandwich and a package of jelly rolls, and a syrup bucket full of water. After several tries, he found a way to tie the spade on the wagon so it wouldn't fall off. The spade was the one his mother used in her garden.

"Did Mamma say you could have it?" Myrtis wanted to know.

"I didn't ast her."

"She gone miss it when she get home."

"Maybe she won't."

Myrtis thought it must be grand to be as old and daring as Dolph. There wasn't a doubt in her mind about his bringing home the gold. Then, of course, it wouldn't matter about borrowing the spade. If only Dolph would let her go along and watch him dig! Or, if only she had the money to dig, herself! She was strong enough to dig up coins. And she could help him load the gold bricks and pull the wagon. But they had already argued this out. Dolph didn't want her hanging around waiting for him all day.

"What if Mamma asts me where you gone?" Myrtis asked.

64

Dolph grinned. "Don't tell no lie. Don't tell her nothing less'n she asts you; then just say I told you not to tell."

The way to the old Perkins farm seemed farther to Dolph this time. Going alone, with the little old wagon rattling behind him and the spade banging against his legs, he was so anxious to get there that he ran part of the way. He was hot and tired and trembling with excitement when he arrived.

There was still a crowd waiting in front of the house, and even more people than before digging in the lot. Dolph made straight for the gate, where a man lounged on an old automobile seat, taking in admission fees. He grinned at Dolph. "You're just in time, Sonny," he said. "Man just walked out of here with a tow sack he could hardly heft."

Dolph paid his money, pulled his wagon through the gate and looked around. At least a dozen men and several women and children were at work. The ground was pocked with holes and trenches. While Dolph stood looking, a shout came from the barn.

A man ran out, holding something in his hand. He waved it and yelled. Some of the searchers dropped their tools and ran to see what he had. Others looked up, but kept on digging. Dolph ran to the barn. He couldn't see what the man was holding, but he heard him say, "It's the sign! It's the sign!"

A woman in front of Dolph asked, "What is it?" Someone answered, "It's just an old arrowhead. That's nothing." The man with the arrowhead cried,

"Madam Astro foretold it! It's a sign!" and rushed back into the barn. The others hurried off to their digging, scattering dirt in all directions.

Dolph ran back to the gate. He had made sure it was the only gate to the cow lot. Madam Astro's words were:

". . . *Add your age and start at the gate.*
Dig, Boy, Dig!"

From his pocket Dolph took two sharp sticks, one tied at each end of a fishing line exactly nineteen feet long. He had added the figures as Madam Astro had told him. Nine for Tory and the pup and ten for his age and that's what they came to. He felt sure that she meant for him to dig nineteen feet from the gate. But which was the starting point? One of the gate posts, or halfway between? He decided on the middle of the gateway, and pushed one of his sticks into the ground there. He stretched the line as far as it would go, and by pressing hard on the other stick and keeping the line taut, drew a semicircle from the fence on one side of the gate to the fence on the other side.

The gatekeeper tried to rattle him. "Just a little more to the right!" He called. "No, I mean left! Hey, you sure that's the spot?" Several newcomers came through the gate and stared. Some asked Dolph what he was doing. Dolph wished they'd all go away and stop bugging him.

He was proud of the semicircle he had drawn on the ground. All he had to do now was dig. But the space he had outlined looked enormous. He had taken it for granted that he was meant to dig at some point nineteen feet from the gate, that the treasure would be along that line. But now it occurred to him that it might just as well be anywhere within the semicircle. He couldn't possibly dig up all that ground in one day. Well, he had to start somewhere. He began along the line next to the fence north of the gate.

When he started to dig, another question arose. How deep ought he to dig? Madam Astro hadn't said anything about that. The grass was as tough as wire. Once he cut through the roots, the earth was fairly soft for a few inches, and then it got hard. The deeper he dug the harder it got. The dirt he lifted out was dry, red and gravelly. When he had a hole two feet deep, Dolph felt as if he had been digging all day.

He stopped and took a drink of water. The bucket was warm from the sun, so he took it out of the wagon and put it underneath. There wasn't any other shade except what he and the fenceposts made. He could tell from the length of these shadows that he hadn't been digging long. He went back to his hole. It looked very, very small.

Dolph dug on. He started another hole beside the first. He decided to dig shallow holes all along the semicircle and then cut between them to make a ditch. That way, he would have a chance to find anything that was near the surface, instead of putting all his chances in one deep hole. It made him feel more like he was getting somewhere.

It was a hot morning, and it got hotter. His hands were sore, and they got sorer. He was thirsty, and the warm water didn't seem to help. Long before noon he had eaten the sandwich and two jelly rolls. Then he was thirstier than ever.

The gatekeeper had brought out a tub full of ice cold drinks. He was selling them for a quarter a bottle! Every time Dolph looked that way, he had a gone feeling in his stomach. He could keep from looking, but he couldn't help hearing the man call out, "COLD drinks! I-C-E cold!"

People came and went, came and went. Dolph could hardly lift his spade. Somebody put a hand on his back and said, "Better go lie down in the shade, kid."

Dolph dragged himself across the grass to the barn and lay down in the narrow strip of shade along one side. How good it felt to stretch out his aching back! The sounds around him—the hum of traffic on the road, voices, the thudding of a pick, the scrape of a shovel, a mockingbird's song, a dirt-dauber's drone, the whirring of small insects in the grass, the faraway hoot of a diesel engine—all blurred and blended, and he was asleep.

XI

THE RAID

When Dolph awoke the shadow cast by the barn had spread. Archie was standing looking down at him, mopping his face with his shirt tail. From the look of him he had been hard at work for some time. Dolph scrambled to his feet. How much time had he slept away? He'd never hear the last of this from Archie.

But Archie was too full of his own troubles to tease Dolph. He rubbed his blistered hands, and said, "It's gotta be a gyp!"

Dolph's back ached, his head ached, and his hands stung; but none of that was as bad as what Archie said. "It ain't!" he cried.

"Well, did you find anything?" Archie sneered.

"No, but I just got started. The gold is there! Madam Astro said—"

"I know what she said. She told me, 'In the corner, under the tree—' Well, I been digging there for a couple of hours." Archie pointed to a corner of the

69

fence where a pile of red dirt lay at the foot of a
young sweetgum tree. " 'You'll be lucky with number
three,' she said. What does that mean? Three feet
from the corner? Three feet deep? Or the third hole
I dig?"

"Well, but—"

"It's gotta be a gyp."

"You just looking for an out, that's you."

"I ain't, either."

"Go on and quit. I'm going to dig some more,"
Dolph said stubbornly. Yet the thought of bending
over that spade again made him sick.

He was still standing looking at the puny piles of
dirt waiting for him by the gate when a stir began
in the yard. Some cars had stopped on the road and
men in uniform were walking toward the house. The
crowd there broke up and scattered as the men ap-
proached. Dolph couldn't see any more; his view was
blocked by the house.

Archie came over. "Hey, what's up?" Others around
them were asking the same thing.

"It's the Sheriff!"

The gatekeeper started toward the house. A woman
ran out of the back door. Car doors slammed and
engines started.

Archie ran for his shovel, went right through the
fence and kept on going. Dolph flew out of the gate
dragging his wagon and spade. Behind him he heard
one of the Sheriff's men shouting, "Take it easy, folks.

Let's keep it orderly. Please vacate these premises in an orderly manner. Madam Astro is no longer in business."

Dolph didn't catch up with Archie until they were halfway home. Archie's legs were longer, and he wasn't burdened with a rickety wagon. When they did meet, they walked along without saying anything. What was the use of talking about what fools they had been?

The long day was ending. They were dirty, hot, worn-out and broke, and didn't have a thing to show for it. They took a short cut across the parking lot of the Kingdom of Heaven Church. Dolph was wondering how he could explain to his mother about the spade, when they came face to face with Brother Biggers.

The preacher was looking at them down his flat nose. Dolph kept his head down. He heard Brother Biggers clear his throat the way he did when he was going to speak. This was it. He was going to ask about the puppies.

"Evening, Boys," Brother Biggers boomed.

Dolph couldn't move. Gooseflesh was popping out on his sweat-soaked skin.

Archie wanted to keep Brother Biggers from asking where they had been. He came out with the first thing he thought of. "Say, what happened with those puppies under the church?"

Hoo, man, Dolph thought. That did it.

71

"You was going to pay us to get them out, remember?" Archie went on, talking fast. "Reckon they still there?"

From what seemed like a long way off, Dolph heard Brother Biggers say, "They gone. Must of left on their own. No thanks to you kids."

"Just my luck," Archie said. "I could have used the pay."

When Brother Biggers and Archie were gone, Dolph sat down on the church steps and grinned into space. He couldn't keep his face straight, he was so glad to have that big load off his mind. Brother Biggers wasn't going to question him about Tory and the pups, after all. The preacher didn't care what happened to them, as long as they were out of his sight. He was satisfied that they were gone, especially since he didn't have to pay a cent to get rid of them. Haw! Haw! Haw!

XII

THE FUNERAL

Dolph was so stiff and sore next morning he hated to move. He sent Myrtis up the hill with some cornbread for the dogs. It was all he had for them. Some of the puppies were beginning to eat soft things like cornbread mashed up in water. The others wouldn't do anything but walk in it.

Myrtis hadn't been away long when she came running back. "You better come," she panted.

"I can't," groaned Dolph, arching his back to show how it hurt.

"You got to." Her eyes were big. "The little white runt pup is dead."

"You sure?"

"He cold."

Dolph started up the street with Myrtis. They climbed the hill almost at a run. Dolph pushed open the door and Tory came to meet him as usual, leaning hard against him and licking his hands with her long,

73

sloppy tongue. She trotted gladly out into the sunshine
and sniffed around in the brush. She was getting more
and more interested in the outside world; more willing
to stay away from the puppies, and for longer at a time.

Inside, six puppies were gathered at the food pan,
three trying to eat from it and three wading in it. The
black puppy was still asleep on the newspapers. The
body of the white pup lay, stiff and swollen, in another
corner.

Dolph felt it and drew his hand back quickly. "We
better bury it."

"We should have brought something to dig with."

Dolph groaned. Dig!

"Let's have a funeral," Myrtis said. "We can play
like the wagon is a hearse. We'll have mourners, and
they got to dress up. I'll get Sarah and Cleon and Barbara and Marvin and Sue Jean. . ."

"You out of your mind?" cried Dolph. "We don't
want nobody to know about Tory and the pups."

"They won't know if we don't tell. All I'll say is, I
found this puppy dead. I did find him, didn't I?"

Dolph was thinking that they could bury the pup
on the lot James owned. There was nothing there but
that old junked car, nobody would care. And it was
far enough away from the shack so that no one would
think of going there.

"Can we? Can we?" Myrtis begged and before
Dolph could stop her she ran down to gather mourners
for the white puppy's funeral.

Myrtis was Funeral Director. She made everyone

74

dress up, even if they couldn't find anything but a ribbon or a scarf or a necktie or a pair of grown-up shoes. Dolph was the preacher. He made Cleon and Marvin dig the grave. They marched along Short Cockleburr Street, singing all the hymns they could remember. The pallbearers carried the coffin box to the grave, and the others stood around it in a circle, waiting for Dolph to do the preacher's part.

Myrtis and the other children were enjoying the game. Dolph wasn't. He didn't feel good about the death of the puppy, and he didn't feel good about the play funeral. He wished he had said a quick no to Myrtis.

He closed his eyes so he couldn't see the neighbor-hood children pretending to be so solemn and grown-up. He spoke fast so he could get rid of them sooner. "Gracious sevenly Father, please bless this little dead puppy," he prayed. They waited for him to say more, but he was remembering how Tory had carried all eight puppies back to safety that night he had stolen them from under the church.

"Amen!" Myrtis said. She was disappointed in Dolph. He wasn't much of a preacher.

The rest of the mourners echoed, "Amen!"

"That's all," Dolph announced. He was the oldest one there, so he could be as bossy as he liked. "Fill in the grave now and go on home."

"I was at a funeral once," Sue Jean said. "The widow, she shouted and tried to jump in the grave with the coffin. It took three men to hold her back."

"My mother knows a woman, when her baby died, she cursed the Lord," Barbara said.

"When my uncle died, there were so many mourners, the cars took an hour driving from the funeral home to the cemetery." Everybody tried to think of a better funeral story than the one before. All but Dolph. He left them chattering and slipped away. Myrtis wanted to follow him, but he made her go back and leave him alone.

He went up a shortcut path beyond James's lot, in the other direction from the shack, and sat under a tree until he saw the children going home. Then he went to the shack and let Tory out. He decided to bring the puppies out, too, for a while. It was so nice outside, so sunny-and-shady, so peaceful under the trees; and they had been shut up so long.

He put them on the ground. They looked like twice as many puppies, stumbling about in all directions, exploring this new world. Tory didn't much like to have them underfoot, but she didn't like it either when they strayed very far from her side. Finally she sat down and let them all gather around her where she could be sure they were safe.

The black puppy, though, didn't follow the rest. She lay still where Dolph had put her. He moved her over with the others, but she didn't seem interested. She just whimpered and panted. Her nose was running, her eyes were sticky, and her paunch was swollen like a balloon.

Like the white puppy was, Dolph thought. She's

76

sick. He hid his face against Tory's warm ears, and cried until he couldn't cry any more.

His mind went round and round, but he could see no way out of his predicament. He felt like the rats he had seen trapped in a wire box at the Corner Store. He remembered their bright, terrified eyes, their twitching ears and whiskers, and their tiny, delicate feet. They had gone into the trap to see what smelled so good in there; then they couldn't get out. Dolph's heart thudded inside his skinny chest. He knew now how they must have felt.

Dolph thought about all this while he lay on the warm sand and sobbed into Tory's ears. Every now and then Tory would lift her head and lick his face. Then she would lay her head down in the crushed grass again, and press hard against Dolph with a long, comfortable sigh.

XIII

THE GIVEAWAY

The puppies were hungry. All the Little Leaveners' good kitchen scraps couldn't seem to fill them up. What the pups wanted was milk, and Tory didn't have any left.

A few days after the white pup's funeral, Dolph watched the puppies try to suck. Tory lay still and let them try, but soon lost patience and walked off. They whimpered and ran after her, all but the black pup, who collapsed where he was. He spit out the cornbread and water Dolph tried to feed him. Next morning Dolph found the black pup cold and limp. That night he was cold and stiff. Dolph wrapped him in some old papers and buried him under the shack.

Then there were only six puppies. Dolph counted them before he left for the night: the black-and-tan, the tan, the black-and-white, the tan-and-white, the black-and-tan-and-white, and the one with leopard spots and blue eyes. Dolph had named them Coonhound, Tansy, Dice, Bubba, Lassie and Lep.

I'll find homes for them, Dolph thought as he squatted on the splintery floor in the corner where the puppies had their bed. They's bound to be people will want puppies.

Tory sat beside Dolph. Lately she seemed more than ready for him to take over the bother of the pups. Dolph hugged her hard. "You my dog," he told her. "My dog and nobody else's. Nobody gone give you away."

The morning after the black puppy died, Myrtis came with Dolph to help feed the dogs. She liked to dress up the puppies and play that they were babies. She had named them Royal, Goldie, Genie, Victoria Junior, Apollo and Jacqueline.

Dolph was in no mood for girl games. Hoo, man, he thought, she gone be just like Janetta and Clara. It came over him with a shock that he and Myrtis didn't quite understand each other the way they used to. Either he was different or she was. He turned on her with a scowl, "Why don't you go on home?"

She looked up at him, surprised. "I'm dressing up Victoria Junior," she held the puppy out for him to see. "Look, ain't she cute, with that bow behind her ear?"

"Go on, take that stuff off," Dolph ordered. "Silly doll games ain't what those puppies need. Use your head. They need to have homes, where they get plenty to eat."

"You going to give them away, Dolph?" Myrtis piped, "When you going to give them away?"

"When I decide, that's when! Go on. Go on home and let me think before I whup you."

Dolph was still thinking that night as he lay on his cot, listening to the sounds of Cockleburr Quarters. He heard the groans of sick old Grandpa Cotten next door, loud laughter and stomping from the Slocum house down the Alley, cars starting off when people left for their jobs on the night shift, and the yowling of cats. None of these familiar sounds ever kept him awake before, and they wouldn't have now if he hadn't been so worried about the puppies.

He thought about how different things were this summer. Not just himself and Myrtis, but Albert, too. Last year Albert would talk to Dolph. He talked mostly about football. He was in training, and jogged to school and back and went to bed early. But during the whole football season Albert never got off the bench. He just didn't have enough beef, the coach told him. That did it, I guess, Dolph thought. That was when Albert declared he was going to quit school. Since then they hadn't seen much of him around home. And even when he came home, he didn't have anything to say to Dolph.

And Janetta. Dolph heard her soft footsteps. She was going out or coming in, he didn't know which. Janetta had a way of slipping in and out of the house so noiselessly that nobody knew in the morning whether she had just come in or just got up. She and Emeline were always quarreling about that.

Emeline and Uncle Leon were quarreling all the

time lately, too. They were at it again right now. Dolph turned over restlessly. Don't I have enough on my mind, he thought, 'thout bothering with other folks' bothers? Hoo, man, Mamma telling Uncle Leon off good! Glad she's not after me.

He turned over on the other side. I'll do it tomorrow, he decided suddenly. Tomorrow morning, I'll start right out and find homes for the pups. Once the decision was made, he rolled himself into a ball and went sound asleep.

The next morning Dolph and Myrtis went up to the shack early. They fed the dogs and let them out to exercise. Three of the puppies were eating for themselves. They wanted all the food and wouldn't let the others come near the pan.

"We'll take the ones that eats good," Dolph decided. "That'll give the puny ones a better chance. You carry Dice and I'll carry Bubba and Lep."

"I'll carry Genie, and you carry Victoria Junior and Jacqueline," Myrtis said. She wouldn't give up the names she had chosen for the pups. Dolph could try to boss her around all he wanted, but there were some things she had to do her way.

They shut Tory in with the three remaining puppies. They could hear her whining and scratching at the door as they hurried off. "Wonder can she count?" asked Myrtis. "Wonder if she knows?"

Dolph didn't want to talk about it. He was wondering why he felt so downright mean about taking away Tory's pups. He wasn't doing anything wrong—not like when he took them away from her before. Then they would have been thrown away. Now they were going to be given to people who wanted them.

They climbed to the top of the hill. Dolph thought it would be better to find homes for the puppies on the other side of the hill, rather than near the Quarters where people might ask questions he didn't want to answer. There were streets of houses just over the top of Cockleburr Hill, beyond the oak grove. Some children he and Myrtis knew from school lived over there.

Dice-Genie, Bubba-Victoria Junior and Lep-Jacqueline nestled, warm and heavy, in their arms. All the pups had big feet and joints, floppy ears, and paunches like footballs. Two such puppies made quite a load to carry. They didn't squirm, though, but seemed content to ride and gaze thoughtfully at everything they passed.

The first street was named Julia (the man who sold the lots named all the streets for his relatives). There were nice, painted houses there, but few people in sight. Dolph and Myrtis went on until they saw a woman in a yard, hanging out wash. A little boy was playing at her feet.

The little boy saw the puppies and started squealing. His mother smiled, so Dolph and Myrtis felt encouraged to go toward them. They put the puppies on the ground and the toddler grabbed for them, squealing louder.

"Tracy, he crazy about puppies," his mother said. "Every one he sees, he goes out of his mind." She watched Tracy fondly as he stumbled after the puppies. Dice-Genie and Lep-Jacqueline tucked their tails under them and ran to the shelter of Dolph's legs. The child caught hold of Bubba-Victoria Junior's tail. The pup squealed as loudly as the child.

"That's the one he wants. Ain't that something?" The woman smiled. "If you're giving them away, that's the one he wants. I can't pay you, but I'll gladly take it off your hands."

Dolph had planned the things he was going to say about taking good care of the pup. But it wasn't easy to tell a grown woman, a stranger, what to do. And what was the use? Grown people did what they wanted, no matter what you told them.

Dolph nodded. Tracy was trying to put Bubba-Victoria Junior upside down into the lady's washbasket. Dolph scooped up the other two pups and ran. When Myrtis caught up, he gave her Lep-Jacqueline to carry.

"What he shivering for?" Myrtis wanted to know.

"Don't bug me," Dolph muttered.

They walked two blocks without saying a word. There were some people at one house they passed, but Dolph didn't stop. They turned the corner and walked down Winnie Street.

A few houses down they met two girls visiting on the sidewalk. One of them, Joyce, they knew by sight; she was a grade ahead of Dolph at school. The girls stopped them to admire the puppies. "Oh, isn't he a doll!" "Oooh, let me hold him! Ain't he something else!" They cooed and danced the puppies in their

84

arms, talking baby talk. When they found out that the puppies were to be given away, they both wanted one.

Dolph said loudly, "You got to take good care of them."

Well! Who wouldn't take care of angel pusses like those? The girls went on and on about how much they loved them. They couldn't wait to show them off at home. They ran down the street, rocking the puppies like babies. Dolph and Myrtis stood looking after them, their arms empty. The last they saw of the two puppies were three floppy ears and a tail.

XIV

THE MYSTERY MAN

Tory seemed restless for a few days; but Dolph and Myrtis couldn't tell whether she was missing the three puppies who were gone or just getting tired of the three who were left. When the hungry pups hung onto her, she turned on them and growled and snapped. She was happy when she could get outside where she could keep out of their way.

"Wisht I could get them some milk," Dolph said one evening, watching the puppies turn away from the bread and water mixture he put down on the ground for them. Tory had gulped down her supper and was sniffing around in the bushes.

"They hands out powdered milk at the Welfare," Myrtis said. "Canned milk, too. That's why Lilboy Wheeler so fat and shiny. The Wheelers, they go to the Welfare every Friday and get butter and sugar and rice and syrup—"

"You know what Mamma says about the Welfare,"

Dolph grinned. "She won't ast favors from nobody, black or white, man, woman, child, Government or the Angel Gabriel."

Myrtis burst out laughing. "Hoo, man. Mamma sure can blister with her tongue."

"Mamma says you ast a favor, might as well hand over your front door key." Then Dolph remembered the sermons Mrs. Randall made him sit through before she gave him work. Maybe that was why Emeline always smiled sourly when he mentioned the Little Leaveners. But Mrs. Randall said, if you don't ask for nothing, you don't get nothing. Dolph didn't know who was right.

When they were ready to leave, Dolph and Myrtis put the puppies back in the shack and called Tory. She didn't want to go back into the hot, smelly room.

"If you didn't have to keep them in there we could clean the shack good and have a nice playhouse," Myrtis said.

"Who wants to play house?" scoffed Dolph, but he was wondering how much longer he could keep the dogs hidden there. The puppies were pining; Tory was fretting; he couldn't make up his mind what to do. He couldn't turn them loose and he couldn't keep them, either.

Myrtis was waiting at the foot of the tumbledown steps, her hands on her hips. "How come you didn't give me some orange?" she demanded. "You're mean. You always keep everything all to yourself."

"Me? What you talking about?"

87

Myrtis pointed at a pile of orange peelings near the shack. They were fresh, neat spirals, cut with a knife, not torn off by hand as they would have done it.

"I don't spend no money on oranges."

"*Somebody* ate oranges, right here. Today."

"Well, it wasn't me, and it wasn't Tory."

The idea of a dog peeling oranges made Myrtis giggle. Then the thought came to both of them: Somebody besides themselves must have been at the shack.

"Reckon did they know Tory was in there?" Myrtis wondered.

"Nobody'd know unless they went inside."

"It might be somebody would steal her."

"Nobody gone steal Tory, her growling and showing her tushes." They better not!

He pulled Myrtis away from the shack. They hid behind some bushes, and watched for intruders. Nothing happened, and after a while Myrtis got tired and went home. Dolph stayed longer, but saw nothing unusual. It looked as if everything were all right, after all.

The next morning when Dolph and Myrtis came up the hill, they stopped again behind the bushes and peered through the leaves. Myrtis whispered, "Let's play Detective."

"Right!" Said Dolph. "I'm the Chief Detective and you're my assistant."

"Right. What we looking for, Chief?"

"Men from Mars."

"Men from Mars!" Myrtis' eyes shone. "Got antennas on they heads and no blood."

88

"And great, big feet. Maybe they inside the shack."

Myrtis jigged with excitement. "Keep me covered, Chief, I'll go look in the windows."

Dolph jerked her back. He didn't want her messing around the shack. Not until he was sure no one was there. "You wait here," he said.

Dolph walked around the shack. There was nobody there. He signalled to Myrtis and opened the door. Tory pushed out, the puppies tumbling behind her. The dogs were always waiting just inside the door now, waiting as eagerly for release as for food. Dolph and Myrtis spread out the scraps on the ground, trying to give an equal amount to each dog. When the scraps were gone, the puppies stumbled around after Tory. Myrtis and Dolph went looking for clues.

They found several. Fresh orange peelings, an apple core, some carrot tops and scrapings of carrot skin. "Maybe the men from Mars is big rabbits," Myrtis giggled.

Dolph found the remains of a fire back of the shack. It had been stamped into the ground, and the ashes were cold. Under the back steps Myrtis found a large can with some brown liquid in it. She sniffed it. "Smells like coffee."

Dolph took the can and smelled it. His eyes grew big. "Coffee."

"Dolph! I hear something."

"Where?"

"Inside the shack."

"Ain't nothing in the shack. You know that." But

89

it occurred to Dolph that he had never looked into the back room. "You stay here and watch," he said. "I'm gone look."

"Don't you do it, Dolph!" Myrtis clung to his arm.

He shook her off. "Anybody hanging around here, I'm gone find out." Dolph crept into the shack. He saw at once that the board across the door into the back room had been pried off. But what really made him stop and stare was Tory's room. It was clean. The dog messes had been scraped off the floor. A nest of clean newspapers was in the corner where the dogs slept. The water pan was clean, and full of fresh water.

What next? Dolph tiptoed toward the back room and listened. There was no sound. He pulled the door open a few inches and peered through the crack. The back room was empty, empty even of trash. The sagging, rotting floor looked as if it had been swept, and a stick with a bundle of twigs tied to one end to make a broom was leaning against the wall. In a corner was a cardboard carton with a rolled-up army blanket on top of it. That was all. Dolph backed out and pulled the door shut.

He heard Myrtis calling, "Dolph! Dolph!" He ran through the shack. "Dolph, come quick! The puppies followed Tory off yonder!" Myrtis pointed into the underbrush.

A man was coming along the faint path. He carried a full paper sack in his arms. In front of him ran Tory, turning and leaping for the sack. The puppies waddled

90

in and out of the path, falling over their own feet. The man stopped when he saw the children, then he came on. Dolph and Myrtis backed toward the shack. They had been taught not to trust strangers, and were ready to run. If the man made a move toward them they had a head start.

The stranger carried his sack to the back steps and sat down with a grunt. Tory came right up between his legs and tried to poke her head into the sack. "Sit, girl, sit," the man said, gently pushing her back. Tory sat, watching his face. The puppies squirmed over his shoes. Myrtis noticed that his toes showed through where the uppers had come away from the soles.

Dolph watched the man, too. He had the look of a tired old hound. Maybe he wasn't all that old; but his forehead was furrowed with deep wrinkles, and the skin of his cheeks hung in folds. He had a little grizzled hair, but was almost bald. He needed a shave. He sat folded up like a pocket knife, as if there were nothing but bones inside his faded khaki clothes. He spoke in a low voice to Tory and the pups.

Suddenly Dolph felt jealous of the way the dogs trusted that man. "That's my dog!" he cried.

The stranger tore the sack down the middle and spread it out on the ground. It was full of all sorts of food scraps. "Ain't much of a life for a dog, shut up in that shack."

Dolph clenched his fists and stuck out his lip. Myrtis said, "Ain't Dolph's fault Tory got to be shut up. Bruh

91

Biggers won't let her stay under the church and Mamma won't let her stay in the Quarters. So we keep her up here, she don't bother nobody."

"Shut up!" Dolph was furious with her for telling a stranger his business.

The man looked off into space. "Well, I don't bother nobody, neither." He tore a slice of bread into three pieces and gave one to each of the pups. "I don't stay nowhere long, then I move on." He turned his mournful hound-eyes on Dolph. "Nothing wrong with that, is they?"

Dolph thought about it. One way you looked at it, it seemed like the man was taking over, interfering. But another way, it looked like he was paying his way. And there wasn't any doubt about how nice he treated Tory. Dolph couldn't see anything wrong with that.

XV

GONE

In just a week or two Dolph and Myrtis were so used to the stranger, it seemed as if he had always been there. However, all they really knew about him was that his name was Jake Brown and that he would soon be moving on. He said he was resting a while. He got his food out of garbage cans behind restaurants and grocery stores. Dolph would be ashamed to do that. He knew what Emeline would say—that only a deadbeat scrounged for food. But Jake said there was a world of good food thrown away every day that ought not to go to waste. He made the rounds of the garbage cans and brought away enough for himself and the dogs.

It was nice for Tory to get the extra food. She already looked a little smoother, not quite so bumpy over the ribs and hip bones. The puppies ate a lot, and their stomachs swelled like balloons, but their backbones showed as plainly as ever. They didn't play much; they just lay around and scratched themselves.

One afternoon Dolph came alone to the shack. He sat with Jake on the steps and watched the puppies sleeping in the shade. Tory sat beside them, her head on Jake's knee. Dolph wondered why Jake looked so mournful. He felt pretty low himself. He still had to find homes for Coonhound, Tansy and Lassie, and he kept putting it off.

"See there?" Jake held Tory's lip up and pointed to her gums. "See how pale her gums are, almost white? They ought to be pink. White gums means bad worms."

"Worms? Where?"

"In her insides. All these dogs ain't been taken care of, they got worms inside that eat up they food and they blood. They never put on flesh, no matter how much you feed them."

So that's why, thought Dolph. All that food for Tory and the pups, and it ain't done them any good. It's all a gyp, a gyp just like Madam Astro. "Ain't there some way to get rid of worms?" he demanded.

Jake hunched his shoulders and shook his head as if bothered by flies. "Sure, they can be got rid of. But it takes time and money."

"I can earn the money. I can. You just got to show me how to get rid of the worms."

"I won't be here that long," Jake said. "I told you that."

"But what about Tory?" Hearing Dolph call her name, Tory turned her one bright eye on him and swept her tail across the ground.

"Don't bug me, Boy." Jake stood up. "All I want is peace and quiet, and all I get is trouble." He shuffled away. Tory, the puppies and Dolph followed at his heels. "Leave me alone," he grumbled, moving on out of sight with his hollow-chested slouch, belt buckle in the lead.

"What you feed her for, if you ain't gone help her?" Dolph yelled after him. "Hunh? Hunh?" There was no answer.

Dolph waited at the shack a long time, until after dark. He waited and thought about the silence and the emptiness, but Jake didn't come back. Finally Dolph shut Tory and her family up for the night and went home.

That night Emeline and Janetta had their biggest fight yet. Uncle Leon was in the middle of it. From his cot on the porch Dolph heard Clara trying to make peace. Then the babies woke screaming and Myrtis took them to bed with her. The people two houses down the Alley came out and yelled for quiet. Dolph turned and burrowed his head into his pillow. The back door slammed. Dolph heard someone go through the yard and then he smelled cigar smoke. Uncle Leon, he thought, drowsily, maybe he gone for good. That'd be the day!

Dolph was sleeping like a log when he was awakened much later by the sound of cars and sirens. Some of the sirens wailed off in the distance, but others were close, and moving closer. Dolph heard people calling out. Bo Slocum came running up the Alley. Albert burst out of the house, pulling on his pants. Dolph hopped off his cot and stammered, "What—what—?"

"Fire! It's a fire!"

"Where at?"

"Look!"

People gathered all along Cockleburr Street, looking toward the dark mass of Cockleburr Hill. Sheets of flame were spread over a wide area and the smoke was just beginning to drift down where they could smell it. A car and a fire truck screeched around the corner of Catalpa Street and roared up Short Cockleburr Street.

Albert cried, "They break their fool necks, they try to drive up the hill that way!" With a crowd of men and boys, he ran toward the hill.

Dolph ran right behind them, wide awake. He didn't think the fire had reached the shack, but he had to make sure. It was like having a nightmare. One moment he was lying on his cot sound asleep; the next he was pounding up the hill, weaving in and out of the crowd, panting hard, his heart shaking his whole body. One moment, Cockleburr Street had been empty; now it was brimming with light and commotion. As Dolph ran, the smell of smoke grew strong and tasted bitter in his mouth. Through the noises of engines and men he could hear a crackling and snapping of flames. The air grew hotter as he climbed. It blew in gusts against his damp skin.

Whistles and shouts came from below where policemen were turning traffic back. Other officers were trying to keep the crowd from going further up the hill.

Most of the spectators stopped, but some managed to get by. They didn't want to miss anything. Nobody noticed Dolph in the half-light, darting like a waterbug from shadow to shadow.

Once past the policeman, Dolph didn't care whether he was seen or not. He ran as fast as he could. The fire engines were working some distance off. Between them and the shack a line of men were clearing away the brush to prevent sparks from setting more of the hill on fire. A bulldozer and some other heavy equipment were waiting at the top of the slope, just in case.

Dolph stumbled toward the shack, yelling for Tory. The doorway was a dark, gaping hole; the door itself was hanging half-off its hinges. Dolph plunged inside. Both rooms were empty.

He ran outside and almost rammed head-on into a man standing with his hands on his hips, looking the place over. The man grabbed him, but his hands slipped off Dolph's bare shoulder. Another man reached out and caught his arm.

"Hey, what you doing here, kid?" They stood over him, one on each side.

"I'm looking for my dog," Dolph said. "Did you see a dog and some pups?"

"Did you see a dog, Sam?"

Sam wiped his smudged face on his sleeve. "No." He called to some other men nearby. "Hey, anybody seen some dogs?"

One of the men turned his head and pushed back his cap. "Is that what they were? I thought they were possums."

Dolph pulled away from the man who held him and ran to the man with the cap. "They was dogs. Where they go?"

"I don't know," the man said. "I heard something in the shack. When I broke the door down, they streaked past me so fast I couldn't shine my light on 'em. I thought I'd got into some kind of a varmint den. Dogs, were they? What were they doing in there?"

Dolph backed away. He looked around. It was growing light. The bulldozer was now being maneuvered down the hill with much roaring and shouting, to push over the shack. The shack was going, just like Jake, just like Tory and the pups. Dolph turned away and tore through the briars and dew-soaked weeds, desperate to get away from the noise and destruction.

"Dolph! Dolph!" he heard Myrtis calling. "Dolph!" She squeezed through a thicket of plum sprouts behind him, her dress wringing wet.

Dolph ran to her and sobbed, "They gone. Tory and the puppies gone."

"We'll find 'em," Myrtis comforted him. "We'll call and they'll hear us. We'll find 'em, Dolph."

Together they worked their way over the hillside, calling, "Tory! Here, Tory! Here, puppy! Here Coonhound! Here, Royal! Here, Tansy! Here, Goldie! Here, Lassie! Here, Apollo!" Dolph whistled until his lips wouldn't pucker. Myrtis had never learned how to whistle. Her piping voice was soon just a croak.

XVI

BUT NOT FORGOTTEN

When Myrtis and Dolph finally gave up and went home, the fire was nearly out. A few grass and brush fires were still smoldering, but there was no further danger to houses or buildings. Everybody had gone home or to work; but the excitement was not quite over.

All Cockleburr Quarters was talking about what Albert had done. Skinny, little, black Albert Burch—yes, that's the one. He was on Cockleburr Hill watching the fire when the man driving the bulldozer went off and left it for a minute with its engine running. That bulldozer took off by itself down the hill, straight for the Fire Chief's new red car. One of the firemen, who was overcome by smoke, was lying on the back seat of that car waiting for the ambulance. There was a dozen grown men standing there watching with their mouths hanging open. They just stood there like stumps. Some of them even shut their eyes, waiting to hear the crash. But not Albert Burch. He saw that thing a-coming, and he went and jumped behind the wheel and swerved it when it wasn't much farther from that red car than the thickness of a coat of paint. You should have seen the look on people's faces when they saw what Albert had done!

You should have seen Albert stop that bulldozer and turn off the switch and climb down like he'd driven those machines all his life! They say the bulldozer driver fainted. When the ambulance came they had to put him in it with the fireman and carry him off to the hospital. They say Albert rode off with the Fire Chief in his red car.

Dolph and Myrtis heard the story from the neighbors on their way home. Myrtis cried, "Hoo, wisht I could have seen old Albert riding in the Fire Chief's car!"

Dolph thought, I could have done the same as Albert if I'da had the chance. If I knew which levers to pull and which pedals to push. How come Albert never showed me all those things about machines? How come Albert's a hero and I'm nothing but Dolph? He was dead tired and miserable. Nothing but Dolph, he kept thinking. Nothing to nobody, except Tory. And Tory's gone.

Their house was empty when they got there. Emeline and Clara were at work and the babies were at the Day Care Center. Janetta and Uncle Leon were nowhere around. Myrtis was so tired she dropped on her bed and went sound asleep. Dolph tried to stay awake to figure out how to find Tory but he couldn't and the next thing he knew his mother was home and the house was full of the neighbors bragging about Albert.

Dolph got sick of hearing about Albert, but Emeline didn't. She didn't take on about it, of course; but her eyes were shining. Every time a visitor told her how the crowd stood waiting for the crash with their faces hanging open, while Albert hopped on the bulldozer and turned the wheel, Emeline would say, "I hear the coffee pot," and go to the kitchen so she could blow her nose.

Dolph woke Myrtis and pulled her out of the house and across the street to sit on the church steps. "We got to find Tory," Dolph said. "You got to help me. Promise." He felt desperate. Jake was gone and Tory was gone and now Albert was a hero. Albert's sudden fame made Dolph feel smaller and lonesomer, somehow.

"I will, Dolph. I will," Myrtis promised. They sat there, not knowing how to start. Finally, Myrtis said, "Let's go tell Miz Randall."

Mrs. Randall! Dolph sprang up and Myrtis followed him down the street.

Like everybody else, Mrs. Randall wanted to talk about Albert. But when she saw the state Dolph and Myrtis were in, she sat down in her rocking chair to listen to their story. The moment they came to a stopping place, she took right over. "All right, now, Dolph," she began, "Ain't a bit of use mourning about

102

what's done. Now you got to turn around and ask people to help you find your dog."

Dolph hurt at the very idea of letting a lot of other folks know about Tory. He shrunk together in his chair, hugging himself.

Mrs. Randall went on, rocking and nodding, "When you lose something, you got to look for it; and the more people looking, the better chance you got to find it. You tell everybody you know to be on the lookout for Tory. They tell everybody they know, and somebody will find her."

"I'll tell all the kids in the Quarters," Myrtis cried. "I'll tell Barbara and Sue Jean and Marvin and Lilboy—"

A little seed of hope sprouted inside Dolph. "Ain't but three ways Tory could go when she run away from the fire," he said. "She either went up the hill, or straight ahead along it, or she come down here somewhere, where people bound to see her."

The old woman nodded. "That's right. That dog ain't gone far from here—not the way you been feeding her."

They decided that Myrtis would go along Catalpa Street, telling all the children she saw about Tory, and Dolph would go up to Julia and Winnie Streets on top of the hill. Before they left her, Mrs. Randall gave them some cold drinks. She sat rocking with her Bible in her lap while they drank, her eyes closed. Dolph and Myrtis thought she was asleep, but the

103

old woman opened her eyes and looked at them over her spectacles. She tapped the book in her lap.

"I been studying," she said. "You know, it's curious, but I been studying the Lord's Word all my life, and I would have stood up in meeting and claimed that I knew it from cover to cover. When you first come to me about Tory, Dolph, I as much as told you that the Bible wasn't for animals, only for people. Yet I could see you had charity in your heart, and the Book says charity will abide." Mrs. Randall rocked as she talked.

"Now, I been studying the Book with new eyes," she said, "And the words just seemed to stand up on the page and speak to me. You know what it says in here, Dolph? It says, 'A righteous man regardeth the life of his beast,' it says. You know what that means? It means if you going to be righteous, you got to look after your dog. And furthermore, it means if you don't look after your dog, you ain't righteous. And *that* means that there's a lot of folks I know calling themselves righteous and looked up to as righteous, who ain't."

Dolph didn't know whether he was supposed to answer her or not. What she was telling him wasn't anything new to him; he had felt it in his heart all the time, and didn't need to read it in a book. Anyway, it wasn't any help in finding Tory. He made a move to go.

"I'm going to pray you find your dog," the old woman said as they left. "Never thought I'd live to see the day I'd pray over a dog. But I'm going to. . . ."

XVII

THE SEARCH

Dolph and Myrtis couldn't start their search for Tory at once, after all. Albert came home in the Fire Chief's car, a sight which all Cockleburr Street gathered to see. The red car stopped in front of the Quarters and the Fire Chief got out and went in the house with Albert to speak to Emeline and shake her hand. After he'd gone, there were so many visitors that Dolph and Myrtis could hardly squeeze into their own house.

Emeline told Myrtis to keep Walter and Harrison out from underfoot. Clara came home, bringing her boyfriend, Pete, and some cakes from the store. She caught Dolph and ordered him to help pass out cakes and coffee to the guests. "Hoo, man, you sure putting it on in front of Pete," Dolph jeered. "Who you think you kidding?"

"All right for you," Clara hissed in his ear, smiling all the while at Pete and the others. "You can mind the babies and Myrtis can pass the cakes. Git." She pushed him out of the room.

Dolph took Walter and Harrison outside and let them play with the hose Emeline kept for watering her garden. If Emeline had seen them she would have had a fit. Perry and Archie came by to hear about Albert. Dolph demanded, "Hey, you seen a dog?"

"I seen a dozen dogs," Perry said. "Hey, is Albert at home? How about that Albert!"

"I mean my dog. You know that mammy dog? About this high—" Dolph tried to describe Tory.

"Did the Fire Chief really bring Albert home?" Perry wanted to know. "Is he going to get a medal?"

"She's lost. I got to find her—"

"Hey, there's old Albert on the porch. Come on, let's ast him how it was."

"Hey, Albert!"

"She's black and brown, got one blind eye—" Dolph was left with his mouth open, while Archie and Perry ran off to the house. "You helping tomorrow, like it or not!" he yelled after them.

Next morning, the search began. Myrtis got Marvin and Cleon and Sue Jean to go up and down Catalpa Street. Dolph and Archie and Perry started up the hill. Quite a few children and some grown people were out, looking at the scene of the fire. The earth was blackened and churned up by vehicles. There was nothing left of the shack but a sheet or two of rusty metal roofing, mangled by the bulldozer, and some splintered boards.

There was no sign of Tory. They called and whistled. Some boys from the other side of the hill asked what they were doing and before long the word spread. Kids all over Cockleburr Hill were yelling and whistling and poking under bushes.

A boy found the body of a dead puppy, run over again and again in the confusion of the fire. It was the black-and-tan-and-white puppy, the one who looked most like Tory, Lassie-Apollo. The poor little crushed body didn't even look like a puppy any more. Dolph felt sick.

A shout went up to the south of them. A dog was running toward them along the side of the hill, with a crowd of boys crashing through the brush behind her, waving their arms and screaming. Dolph yelled, "Tory! Tory!" but he couldn't make himself heard above the racket. "Don't," he screamed. "Leave her be!" But the boys paid no attention. They were having too much fun.

It was Tory, all right. Dolph got one good look at her as she streaked across a clearing and disappeared into a thick briar patch. By the time he and his friends reached the place, Perry and Archie were hot and winded and ready to give up.

Dolph left them behind. He struggled along the edge of the thicket, sobbing with anger and frustration. If he had only kept quiet and gone alone to find Tory! Now she might never come back. And he might never know what happened to Coonhound and Tansy. Dolph went on and on, looking for Tory, looking and calling, until he was so hot and thirsty and scratched he didn't think he could make it back to the Quarters.

During the days that followed, Dolph searched constantly for Tory. There were rumors that she had been seen. Mr. Speck thought he saw Tory one morning over on Maxwell Street, but when he turned around and went back there was no dog in sight. Mrs. Whitaker phoned to say there was a stray dog in her backyard, but it wasn't the right color or size. One of the workmen at the Housing Project was bitten when he tried to catch a dog he thought might be Tory.

A week went by with no success. Myrtis had tried hard, too, with no luck—but she did get an idea. She remembered what Mrs. Randall had said about praying to find Tory. If Mrs. Randall could get what she wanted by praying, why couldn't they?

Myrtis and Dolph had heard preachers pray. They knew a lot of words, but they weren't sure just how to put them together right. They wanted to do it right. This wasn't a child's game, like the white puppy's funeral.

They sat on their porch Prayer Meeting night and listened to what was going on at the Kingdom of Heaven Church. Brother Biggers' voice came booming out across the street. The congregation rumbled back at him: Amen. That's right. Yes, Lord! Amen.

"If we use enough amens, we be O.K.," Dolph decided.

"You do the praying and I'll do the amening," Myrtis said.

109

Dolph thought a while, then he prayed, "Our gracious sevenly Father—"

"Amen!"

"God bless thy straying lost lamb, Tory—"

"Say Victoria. Say Gloria Victoria, it sounds better. But she's no lamb."

"She is when you pray. You just stick to amening, Sis' Myrtis—"

Myrtis giggled.

"If you can't pray right—" Dolph snapped.

"I'll pray right, Dolph. Amen!"

"Bless thy straying lost lamb Victoria, then," Dolph went on. "And help this poor sinner to—Say amen, can't you?"

"Amen! Yes, Lord!"

"—to find her soon. And the puppies. Amen."

"Amen."

They were singing along with the congregation when they heard a stir down the street, voices and running footsteps. A small crowd was coming along the sidewalk. Dolph and Myrtis ran out to look.

They saw a man leading a dog toward them. No; it was the dog who was leading the man, dragging him forward at the end of a rope. The man was Jake Brown, and the dog was—"Tory!" Dolph yelled, "Tory!"

Tory pulled the rope out of the man's hand and charged into Dolph's arms.

110

XVIII

HOME

"Where'd you find her, Jake? Where'd you find her? Where the puppies?"

Jake told about finding Tory hiding in a pile of brush at the far end of Cockleburr Hill. There was one dead puppy with her. He couldn't find any more. "She wouldn't come out for the longest, even when she knew it was me," Jake said. "The sirens and bulldozers and the fire scared her so bad; and then when she came out later, folks chased her. She had a rough time."

Dolph took a good look at Tory. Man, was she skinny! Why, she looked worse than when she was nursing the puppies under the church. He'd have to feed her up again. And find out what to do about those worms.

But where could he keep Tory now? If only his mother would let him keep her here! But it wasn't likely that Emeline would change her mind about

111

dogs. Still, it wouldn't hurt to ask her. She was feeling so good about Albert, there was just a chance. . . .

Emeline came outside with Clara and Albert to see what was going on. Dolph could tell from the expression on his mother's face that she didn't think much of Jake's looks. He tugged at Jake's sleeve. "Tell her, Jake. Tell how you hunted and hunted for Tory, and finally found her."

Jake wasn't much help. "You done told her," he said.

Dolph looked at his mother. It was now or never. "I can keep her here, now, can't I, Mamma?" His voice sounded funny and squeaky.

Emeline threw up her hands. "You out of your mind?"

"She's my dog." Dolph stuck out his lip.

"Well, she ain't mine," Emeline said. "You know I don't allow dogs on my place, digging up my garden."

"Tory don't dig, Mamma. She's crippled."

"She'll mess, then."

Jake made a move to ease himself away. Emeline stopped him. "Don't you walk away from here and leave that dog," she warned. "You brought her. You can take her away."

"Miz Burch—" Jake drew his chin down between his shoulders.

Myrtis piped up, "Mamma, Tory's a nice dog. She don't bark a bit. She—" But Emeline wouldn't listen to her, either.

Then Albert spoke up. "Aw, Mamma, why don't you let Dolph keep the dog a while, see if she do any harm."

"Harm? She hopping with fleas."

"Yeah, but fleas don't bite on people when they got a dog to bite."

Dolph's mouth hung open. Albert on his side, speaking up for him. And Emeline listening to Albert like he was a grown man. But she turned back to Dolph and said, "Dog that size, how do you expect to feed her?"

Albert said, "Dolph's been earning, Mamma; he can buy food. And I can help him if he needs it. I got me a job today."

"You did!" Clara broke in. "You got that filling station job?"

"Sure did. I went and ast for it and they hired me right off." Albert grinned. "They ast me if I knew anything about ordinary cars; said I wouldn't have much call for driving bulldozers."

Everybody laughed. Emeline, too, but she hadn't forgotten about Tory. She laid down the law while Dolph, Myrtis, Jake and Tory listened with hanging heads. "No dog lives on my place, Dolph. I can't help it if you want to feed her, but if she pokes her snout inside my clean house, or messes in my garden—"

"Aw, Ma. . . ."

The bystanders lost interest and drifted away. "I'm sorry, Dolph," Emeline said. "That's the way it's got to be." She went inside. Clara said she was sorry too and Albert thumped Dolph on the head. Once Eme-

line Burch made up her mind there was nothing anybody could do.

Jake Brown stood in the yard with Dolph and
Myrtis, looking down at Tory. Finally he muttered,
"Well, so long."

So long? Dolph grabbed his arm. "Where you going, Jake?"

Jake hunched his shoulders and shuffled off. Tory
waited, looking at Dolph, then got up uncertainly and
limped after Jake. Halfway down Cockleburr Street,
Jake turned and saw her following him. "Go back!"
he told her. She sat down. Jake pointed back and com-
manded sharply, "Go back!"

Tory looked at Jake, both ears pressed down. Then
she trotted slowly back toward Dolph and Myrtis.
Dolph choked. Tory couldn't stay with him. He had
to send her away. He pointed as Jake had done and
tried to copy his tone of command. "Go—!" But
Dolph's voice broke. He couldn't chase Tory off. He
couldn't.

Jake was still in sight, shuffling along the walk in
front of Mrs. Randall's house. Dolph ran to catch up.
Myrtis ran behind him, and Tory was right at their
heels. Dolph called, "Jake! Jake!" The man stopped,
turned and waited. But when the children came near,
Dolph couldn't think what to say.

"Well, what you want?"

"Jake, where's Tory going to go, hunh?"

"Goshsakes! How do I know?"

114

"We chase her away, she'll go back to the brush-pile," Dolph had to make him understand.

"What you expect me to do?" Jake said. "I ain't got nowhere to keep her."

"She'll starve to death!" Myrtis mourned.

Tory was nosing around the steps of the house next door to Mrs. Randall's. It was the last in the row of rent houses, and it was empty. The family who had been living there had moved out the week before. Tory found a bone that still had a smell of meat on it. She stretched out on the bottom step and held the bone down with her front paws and gnawed it, keeping her eye on Jake and the children.

Myrtis said, "Dolph—!" She took Jake's hands and pulled him toward the house.

"Now, look!" Jake protested.

"It's empty, Jake," Myrtis told him. "How about that!"

Dolph beamed. How about that! An empty house, just when Jake and Tory needed it.

Jake held back. "I can't pay rent."

"Rent collector don't come around till Saturday night!"

Dragging Jake between them, the children pushed the door open and peered into the dark, empty room. "It ain't no palace," Jake said.

Dolph and Myrtis thought this was hilarious. They had been so scared and sorry, the relief was like taking the lid off a boiling kettle. They squealed and fell

115

against each other and rolled on the dusty floor. They hugged Jake. They hugged Tory.

Jake heaved a long sigh. "Lord, Lord!" He pushed them out the door. "Git along now. Git along home," he growled. "See you tomorrow."

"We certainly will!" Dolph led the way home, chanting, "See you tomorrow! Certainly will! Certain-ly, cer-tain-ly, cer-tain-ly willll!" Myrtis chimed in. Tory hesitated, wanting to follow Dolph. Jake called her, and she went back to her bone.

XIX

MOUTHS TO FEED

It was a long time before Dolph went to sleep that
night. He couldn't believe that Tory was really found.
And safe, at least for now. He slept late. When he
woke, the hot sun was bearing down. The house was
empty. Neither Janetta nor Uncle Leon had been back
since the quarrel. Clara and Emeline had left for
work, taking the little ones with them. Myrtis had
gone to the Corner Store. Dolph pulled on his jeans
and ran to Jake Brown's house.

Tory was lying on the porch, her head across Jake's
feet. When she saw Dolph coming she jumped up
and ran limping to meet him. Then she led him back
to where Jake sat leaning against the wall in the sunshine, his knees under his chin. He said he was waiting until the breakfast business at the restaurant on
Maxwell Street was over. Then he would check their
garbage cans; ought to be something good there. Next,
he would try the cans behind the supermarket. If he

didn't find enough at the back door, he'd walk right in the front door and ask for stale bread. He could always get a good breakfast that way. But it was different with Tory. "Bread and doughnuts ain't what she needs," he said, looking at her mournfully. "She needs real dog food, plenty of it, and regular."

"I got a dollar saved. I'll earn enough more to buy a sack of dog food—a big sack. Hoo, man! Tory never had a whole sack of dog food."

Dolph saw Mrs. Randall walking in her yard, looking Jake over. She never missed much that went on in the neighborhood. Dolph ran to the fence. He explained about Jake finding Tory and asked her for some work to do but Mrs. Randall was suspicious. She cautioned him not to trust Jake too far. "He toils not, neither does he spin," she said, not troubling to lower her voice, "But that don't make him a lily. Just you keep that in mind."

"Yes'm." Dolph asked again about the errands, and the old woman went in her house, shaking her head, to telephone her friends. Dolph ran home for his wagon, and set out to earn the price of a big sack of dog food for Tory.

When Emeline came home after lunch, Dolph was waiting to give her his earnings. He watched her, big-eyed, hopping from one foot to the other, to see how much she would give him back. She put some coins into his hand, looked at his hot, wet face and added a dollar bill. "Go ahead," she told him, with her sourest smile, "Go ahead and waste your money on that dog. You'll learn."

Dolph ran to the Corner Store and came rattling back with the dog food sack bouncing in the wagon. While he was gone Jake had brought his army blanket and grocery carton from wherever he had hidden them. He had swept out the house with an old thrown-away broom he had found. And some of the children, playing nearby, had gathered to watch the goings-on.

Dolph was going to tear open the sack and let Tory have it all, but Jake stopped him. "Won't do her no good to gorge herself," he said. "She been empty so long, make her sick to eat too much at a time. Get a pan and I'll show you how much to give her."

Dolph started off to his house. Myrtis cried, "Mamma skin you, you take one of her pans!"

"She's out back in the garden."

"Never mind where she's at; she'll know."

Jake told them to look around the yards. There was plenty of trash there. The children didn't have far to go before finding several things that would do. They brought their loot to Jake: a hubcap, a washpan, three TV Dinner trays and a burnt-out roasting pan.

Jake selected the washpan for a waterbowl and the hubcap for a feeding pan. Dolph was tearing into the feed sack again when Jake ordered, "Wash the pans, first."

The children stared. "Wash?"

"Wash. With soap."

119

Cleon burst out laughing. "Wash dishes for a dog?" Everybody giggled.

"Dirt and germs hurt dogs just like they do you," Jake said. "Besides, could have been poison in those pans."

"Poison? You kidding."

"No sir," Jake said. "Why, they's poison all over the place. Rat poison, roach poison, weed killer, gasoline—" Their eyes grew bigger at each poison he named.

"Man come through the other day with the skeeter sprayer," Dolph said. "That's poison, ain't it?"

"You better believe it. So wash the pans."

"Myrtis, you and Sue Jean go wash the pans," Dolph ordered, copying Jake's tone of authority.

Tory was pawing impatiently at the feed sack when they were finally ready to feed her. She drank most of the water as soon as they put it down. "Fill it," Jake directed, "and keep it filled. She needs lots of fresh water, weather like this."

"Fill the water bowl," Dolph told Myrtis.

Jake measured a heap of food chunks into the hubcap and Tory wolfed them down.

"Can't she have some more? She hungry."

"Give her that much again tonight. Feed her twice a day for a while till she catch up."

The mangy dog who hung around the Wheeler house and the shaggy dog who slept under the Slocum house were watching all this. They crept as close as they dared. Tory growled at them, guarding her empty

120

pan. A chunk or two of food that had spilled on the ground tempted Shaggy. He inched forward on his belly, sniffing the good smell. Dolph kicked at him, missed, and picked up a bottle to throw. Marvin and Cleon yelled to help chase Shaggy away.

Jake Brown seized Dolph's arm. "You hit that dog with that bottle, I'll thump your head till it jerks like a jackhammer."

Dolph gaped at Jake. He hadn't thought the man could move so fast or grip so strong, much less talk so fierce. "But they after Tory's food!"

Jake's dark eyes were fixed directly on Dolph's. "They hungry," he said.

"But— But they ain't *my* dogs!"

"So what?" Jake repeated, "They hungry."

"But they'll eat up Tory's good store-bought food!" wailed Dolph. He understood what Jake was telling him, all right, but he didn't want to listen.

"Hungry is hungry," Jake said.

Dolph kicked over the feed sack and yelled, "Take it, then. Give it all away, see if I care!" He stormed into the house.

Through the screened door he watched Jake pour dog food into the hubcap while the mangy dog and the shaggy dog emptied it twice each. Then Jake rolled the top of the feed sack down to close it and sent the children to look for a can to keep what was left, safe from ants and roaches and rats. By this time, all the children in Cockleburr Quarters were there to see what was going on.

121

XX

WAR ON WORMS

Saturday evening, when the rent collector came around, the children warned Jake Brown. He disappeared from the Quarters until the collector had gone. Since Jake had no furniture nor extra clothes nor things to cook with, his house looked just as empty as it had before he came. On Sunday morning Jake and Tory were back sitting on their steps.

Mrs. Randall warned Dolph again about Jake. She said he was a loafer and a squatter and nobody knew what else. Anybody could see that sooner or later he would mean trouble. "Don't your mother tell you that?" she asked.

"Yes'm; but she's swapping him cooked greens and cornbread for working in her garden."

Mrs. Randall snorted. "Emeline would put up with the Devil himself if he carried a garden hoe." She demanded, "How long he expect to live in the Quarters rent free? How long he expect to live on greens and cornbread?"

Dolph didn't know. But Mrs. Randall never gave up. The next time she saw Jake sitting on his porch with Dolph and Myrtis and Tory, she marched across her back yard and stood at the fence to quiz him.

Jake listened to her, sitting the way he did, like a folding chair folded up. He didn't know how long he was going to stay, he said. How was he going to live? Well, he was doing all right. Why didn't he get a job? It didn't seem hardly worth while to get a job when he'd be moving on soon.

Dolph didn't like to hear Jake talk about moving on. And he wasn't the only one who liked Jake. Tory liked Jake. All the youngsters in the Quarters liked him—he somehow made life more interesting. Even Emeline said he was a good hand in the garden. Dolph wished Mrs. Randall would leave Jake alone. He tried to change the subject.

"Jake says Tory got worms," he said. "He says they's pills you can get will kill them. When the worms is gone, she'll get the good out of her food; she'll get fat and sassy. But we ain't got the money yet to buy the pills."

"You and your Tory, you and your worms!" Mrs. Randall grumbled. "If you listened to the Lord's Word like you listen to Jake Brown, you'd be better off."

"I do listen! I listen to you when you talk about the Book, and I listen to Jake when he talks about Tory."

To Dolph's surprise, Mrs. Randall threw her head back and laughed—a good, loud laugh. "You do beat all," she told Dolph. "You just busting with bright ideas and you don't even know it."

"Me?" Dolph stared at Mrs. Randall, and Myrtis stared at Dolph, hoping to see a bright idea bust out.

"Yes, you." She chuckled. "Tell you what I'll do. You bring me some of these kids I see hanging around the Quarters just looking for trouble. You bring 'em to my place and I'll tell them a story from the Bible. You do that, and I'll pay for the worm pills."

Dolph turned to Jake and Jake nodded. "You do what Miz Randall says, I'll stay long enough to worm Tory."

That very afternoon Dolph went through the Quarters banging on a pan. When the kids came running, he started to chant as much like the man he had heard at Madam Astro's as he could. He called out:

Story time! Story Time!
Tell you a story, won't cost you a dime.
World-famous story teller! Straight from the Book!
Free refreshments! You don't have to cook.
Come one! Come all!

The boys and girls crowded around him, wondering if he'd gone crazy. Dolph led them at a gallop along the sidewalk to Mrs. Randall's.

The old woman gasped when she saw them coming. She threw up her hands and Dolph was scared for a minute that he had done the wrong thing. But she held the screened door open and let the children inside.

124

Next day all the kids in the Quarters gathered to see Jake worm Tory. Jake showed them the worm capsules. He had walked across town to the Animal Hospital to buy them. They were pretty, like red jelly, but Jake said they were poison. "Have to be, to kill worms," he explained. "That's why you got to use just the right amount. Use too many, you kill your dog along with the worms. Leave them lying around where the baby eat them, you kill the baby."

The amount you gave depended on the weight of the dog. Jake said Tory weighed about thirty pounds, so he had bought a twenty-five pound capsule and a five pound capsule. Giving them was simple. He rolled each one in a little ball of hamburger and held it out to Tory on the flat of his hand. Tory hadn't had any breakfast, because the worm medicine worked best on an empty stomach. Those hamburger balls disappeared as fast as if Tory had been a vacuum cleaner. The boys were disappointed. "Is that all? Is that all you do?"

"Some dogs won't gulp they food. They tear the hamburger apart and spit out the medicine," Jake answered. "Dog like that, you have to put the pills down his throat. But these hungry-type dogs, they not going to spit out nothing."

The mangy dog and the shaggy dog were sniffing at his legs. The smell of the hamburger was stronger than their fear. A black mammy cat and her two-half-grown yellow kittens were crouched under the steps, waiting to come out when the dogs went away.

125

Mrs. Cotten stood in her doorway watching. She laughed. "I told you what would happen if you started feeding strays. What's more, they'll be coming here from miles around looking for a handout. Too many around here already, if you ask me."

Jake stood watching the hungry dogs and cats, and the children watched him. They would have chunked the strays away, but they knew Jake wouldn't let them.

"It's easy to give away feed other folks buy," Mrs. Cotten called. "When you going to get a job yourself?"

Jake didn't answer her. He spoke to the kids. "You know, Mangy and Shaggy here, they got worms, too. So do the cats."

Lilboy Wheeler piped up, "Fishing worms?"

The others shrieked with laughter. The children a few years older than he, feeling a whole lot wiser, pranced around chanting, "Fishing worms! Fishing worms!" and pretending they were going to die laughing.

The biggest boy there was Bo Slocum. He seldom paid attention to the younger kids, but today he had stayed at home to find out what was going on. "I ain't seen no worms," he challenged Jake.

Cleon and Marvin were thinking the same thing. They had hoped for worms as big as snakes, squirming every whichway and making the girls squeal.

"Don't have to see them to know they's there," Jake said.

126

"How do you know?"

Jake explained about pale gums being a sign of worms. Bo interrupted, "Me look inside dog and cat mouths? I know better than to get bit that way."

Jake nodded. "It don't do to go fooling around an animal ain't used to your handling. You have an animal, you ought to get him used to being brushed and looked at and treated. You ought to know what a healthy animal looks like. You, Boy; you never saw a healthy dog or cat around here in your whole life."

"Hey, man—!"

Jake repeated, "You never saw a healthy dog or cat around here. Look at 'em! Look at that dog. Look at that cat. You can take my word for it, they all got worms."

Dolph bragged, "Tory ain't got worms now!"

"It takes the medicine a while to work, Dolph. Besides, it takes more than one dose to get all the worms. And even then, she's just going to pick up some more."

"How come?"

"Worms live in the ground. Every place a wormy dog or cat makes a mess, worms and worm eggs going to grow."

"But I thought—"

"Makes no difference what you thought. That's the way it is."

Some of the youngsters were giggling and pointing at dog and cat messes they saw on the ground. Bo made loud noises, Haw! Haw! Haw!

127

It was no joke to Dolph. "All this ground got worms in it, how we going to cure Tory?" When Jake didn't answer, Dolph pulled at his sleeve. "You said you could make her fat and sassy!"

The wrinkles in Jake's forehead deepened. He hunched his shoulders. "Now, look here—"

"Well, you can, can't you? You told me you could." Dolph kept after Jake.

Finally, Jake mumbled, "You got to worm the lot of them, Boy—not only Tory, but Mangy and Shaggy and the cats. You got to pick up after them, and pick up after every dog and cat comes messing around the Quarters. That's what you got to do. Now, who's going to do that?"

"How you mean, pick up? You mean—?" The kids were giggling again.

"Yeah, that's what I mean." Jake looked down at the surprised faces. The children didn't know whether he was kidding them or not. They didn't know whether to be amused or insulted. What he said was as strange to them as a foreign language. Their expressions were so comical, Jake's wrinkles spread and the loose skin of his cheeks shook. He was laughing. "Go get me a spade," he told them between chuckles. "Get me a spade and a bucket, and I'll show you how to get ahead of them worms."

XXI

THE FLEA FIGHT

The boys and girls in Cockleburr Quarters had never had so much fun. Those who could find a spade or a bucket ran from one yard to the next, picking up dog and cat droppings. "Here's one! Yonder's another! Hey, man, here's the biggest one yet!"

What grown people were at home couldn't believe their eyes. Mrs. Wheeler and Mrs. Cotten tried to call their children home, but they got to laughing so hard they gave up. Marvin's grandfather groaned and carried on about the noise. Bo's big sister hid their spade so he wouldn't find it; but Bo took a piece of tin and a broom handle and made himself a pickup tool that worked better than a spade. He showed off his invention to everybody who would look. He said he was going to get it patented.

Dolph bossed all the kids younger than he and Bo bossed the rest. Jake came along behind them with a sack of lime he had found under his house. He let the children who said they couldn't stand the sight of a mess take turns spreading lime on the ground where each mess had been. He said it ought to be salt to kill the worms in the dirt, but the lime would keep away the flies. Jake showed where to empty out the buckets, at the back of the yards, against the Project fence.

"We could bury it," he said, "but spread it out like this and cover it up good with lime, won't be no flies nor odor." And there wasn't.

They found lots of other things while they were searching for droppings. Marvin found a long piece of chain. He showed it to Jake. "We can use it to tie up Mangy and Shaggy the night before you worm them," he said. "You said you had to tie them to make sure they don't eat nothing."

"Right," said Jake. "But it won't do to chain them around the neck. They could cut themselves bad that way, not used to being tied and pulling to get loose. See if we can't find an old belt or something made of leather. We'll make collars for them."

Jake certainly did know a lot about dogs. He thought of things a dog might do that nobody else would have thought of. Dolph couldn't help worrying about what would happen when Jake moved on. Where could he keep Tory then? How could he take care of her? Hoo, man! Looks like the more you learn, the more you need to know. "You'll never teach a dog nothing if you ain't smarter than the dog," Jake said.

When they looked carefully among the trash for

130

pieces of leather, there was no end to the things they found. They found some bottles they could return to the store for money. They began putting things they could use or sell in one pile and useless trash in another.

"I know a man used to make a living selling stuff he found at the dump," Bo said. "Betcha we could make enough out of this junk to—"

"To buy worm pills for Mangy and Shaggy—"

"And the cats—if we can catch them."

"Cost a lot."

They gathered around Jake. He spread out his empty hands. "Sure, it'll cost. What's more, we need some dip to kill the fleas on these dogs. That costs, too." Tory and Shaggy and Mangy spent half their time scratching themselves.

When there was a good pile of bottles, Dolph called his crew together and announced, "We got priority on the bottles!" It sounded so good that nobody disputed his claim.

Bo cried, "Well, then, we got the scrap iron concession. That man I know, he'll buy it. Hands off the scrap iron, everybody!"

The bottle business and the scrap iron business lasted for days. The scrap iron man came and hauled off a sizeable load. Somebody had the idea of making FOR SALE signs to stick up by the piles of salvage. People passing along the street stopped to look, and sometimes they bought things. The children argued about the money they made, until it was agreed that they would hand it over to Mrs. Randall to hold for them. Jake wouldn't take it. He said he had holes in both pockets, money wouldn't stick.

Mrs. Randall took their money and handed it back again to buy what the dogs and cats needed. It paid for dip to kill ticks and fleas. Dipping the three dogs took most of one morning. Jake mixed the stuff in a tub with half cold and half hot water. He wouldn't let anybody else do it because he said the dip was poison. More poison! Got to be to kill the fleas. He screwed the top tight on the bottle and put it in his hip pocket.

He stood Tory in the tub and let Dolph and Myrtis help ladle the dip over her. Afterward, he made them wash their hands and arms with soap.

Tory didn't mind being dipped as long as Dolph was with her. Jake showed how to wet her head without letting the dip get inside her eyes and ears. The children squealed with excitement to see the fleas hopping and scurrying in all directions. There were dead fleas floating on the water. Hoo, man, thought Dolph, bet those fleas think the giants are after them for sure. Myrtis was thinking the same thing.

The water was mud-colored when they finished dipping Tory. Jake put a rope on the collar Dolph had made for her, and told him to keep her on the porch until she dried, so she wouldn't go and rub in the dirt. "Let her shake all she wants," he said, and did she shake! The water flew all over the porch. Jake said it was a good thing. Fleas lived off of a dog as much as on him, and they might be sitting in the cracks be-

132

tween the boards just waiting to jump back on Tory when the dip wore off. He poured the dirty dip on the ground under the porch to kill any fleas that might be living there. He made sure it all soaked into the dirt.

Dipping Shaggy and Mangy wasn't so easy. Shaggy let Jake put a rope around his neck, but it was the first time he had ever felt a rope, and it scared him to death. He fought like crazy. The boys yelled, the girls squealed, and the women came to their doors to see the excitement.

Jake seized Shaggy by the scruff of his neck and, holding the dog's head away from him, put his other hand under Shaggy's chest and lifted him into the tub. After thrashing around a few moments, Shaggy gave up. He crouched in the tub, rolling his eyes and shivering. Jake kept a tight grip on the back of his neck while Marvin and Bo poured dip over him.

"O.K.!" Marvin cried. "Next!"

"Not so fast, Boy." Jake parted Shaggy's fur. Under the top mats it was still dry and full of active fleas. "Them fleas just laughing at us," Jake said. "We ain't even seen the color of Shaggy's hide. This dog could have a message wrote on his skin and we'd never know it."

Dolph and Myrtis tied Tory on the porch and came running to look. All the children hung over the tub. Bo's big sister called out to know what had happened.

"We looking for a secret message!" Sue Jean called back.

"You got to be kidding."

"An enemy agent might have wrote a message on Shaggy's hide," yelled Cleon.

"So nobody could find it."

"It's a secret formula." Everybody had ideas.

"It's wrote in invisible ink, and we can't read it till it's good and wet."

Grandpa Cotten pulled himself up in bed so he could look out of his window. "What those kids jabbering about?"

"That screwball Jake Brown, and his screwball notions."

"Sounds like a jaybird convention."

Dolph pulled at Shaggy's hair. Besides the fleas, there were grassburrs, and black specks which Jake said were made by fleas, and ticks. Jake turned back one of the dog's ears. Inside the flaps more ticks were clinging. Some were buried deep into the flesh, others were so swollen that they dropped off at a touch and went plop! into the water. Some children screamed and rushed away. Bo's sister went back into her house, slamming the door.

Jake, squatting by the tub, said, "This dog's been in misery long enough. Coat like this needs to be combed out and brushed. It'd take a week's hard labor to do that." Dolph watched and waited. Jake growled, "You bugging me, Boy."

"No I ain't, Jake," Dolph protested. "I'm just watching."

Jake hunched his shoulders. After a while he said, "Well, I guess I could give Shaggy a haircut."

134

Hoo, man! Give a dog a haircut. The kids hung onto each other to keep from falling down laughing.

Shaggy had too much hair, but Mangy was almost naked. What hair Mangy had was short and thin. There were patches of sore-looking bare skin around his eyes and mouth, on his paws and under his neck. When Shaggy was out of the tub, and tied on the porch of a house where nobody was at home to object, Jake put Mangy in for his dip. Mangy didn't fight the rope. He had learned that Jake gave him food and never threw things at him. So he let Jake pick him up, but he made himself as heavy as he could and pressed hard against the far side of the tub.

"Mangy dog! Mangy dog!" Lilboy Wheeler started the chant and the other little ones took it up.

Sue Jean and Myrtis had been ready to help dip Mangy, but now they jerked their hands back.

"Mange won't hurt you," Jake told them. "Mangy mites spread around among dogs. People ain't likely to get 'em."

"You going to cure Mangy's mange?" Myrtis asked. She still wasn't sure she wanted to touch the dog.

"Mange is sometimes mighty hard to cure." Jake muttered. "There's different kinds of mange, and different medicines for each kind. A lot depends on the dog, does he get good food and does he have fleas."

It was easy to see the fleas scatter through Mangy's sparse hair. There were ticks inside his ears, too, and sore spots outside where he had scratched.

"Scratching fleas and ticks is what give those old

135

mangy mites a chance to dig into a dog's skin," Jake said. "That and being wormy and not getting fed right."

"Let me see the mangy mites!" cried Lilboy.

"Where? Where?" The others crowded close.

"You can't see them. But mangy mites, they's every-where dogs are. Generally they leave the clean, healthy dogs alone; just pick on the puny ones."

"We get the fleas and ticks off Mangy, will he get well?"

"He might. Sometimes a good dip will start the skin to heal right away. It's worth trying."

Dolph and Myrtis and Marvin helped Jake pour the dip over Mangy. Jake pulled off the biggest ticks, but he said it was better to wet the ticks good with the dip and let them fall off later by themselves. That way they wouldn't leave raw, sore places.

"Let's dip the cats!" Marvin cried when all the dogs were dipped.

"You don't dip cats."

"They got fleas, ain't they?"

"They got fleas, but you use something special for cats. Stuff that'll do for a dog will poison a cat. Any-way, stick a cat in the water, it'll scare him to death."

"Aw, come on!" Bo grinned. "Let's try it!"

Jake fixed Bo with his dark, mournful eyes. "It don't take brains to torment an animal. It takes brains to learn their ways." He turned away from Bo. "Tell you what, the first one to figure out the right way to deflea a cat, I'll give 'em a prize."

XXII

FAT AND SASSY

It was no trick at all to worm Mangy and Shaggy. They both gulped down their capsules at once. But worming the cats was a different matter. Nobody had ever petted or handled the black mammy cat. She wasn't about to let herself be caught; and she had taught her yellow kittens to do as she did.

The boys wanted to chase them into a corner and grab them, but Jake told them that would just be showing off their ignorance. All they would get would be scratched hands, and the cats would be wilder than ever. "You can kill a cat, but you can't man-handle him," he said. "I'll show you a better way to catch them."

He walked all the way to the Animal Hospital again and came back with three traps he had borrowed from the veterinarian. They were wire-mesh boxes, each just big enough to hold a cat. You put food at one end and set the door open at the other end so the

138

cat would go in to get it. When he went in, the door snapped shut and the cat was a prisoner.

"I sure hate to do this," Jake growled. "I been behind bars, myself." He rubbed his forehead with both hands, as if to wipe something out from deep inside his head. "Difference is, a man knows what he's put in jail for. A man's supposed to know what he's doing; cats ain't."

"What you going to do with them when you catch them, Jake?"

"I'll take them to the veterinarian, for him to worm. He knows how to do it 'thout hurting. I sure hate to scare 'em like this." He muttered, "Cats and dogs both ought to be handled kindly when they's little, save all this trouble later on." He set the traps under the house where the cats usually stayed, then called the dogs and children away to wait out of sight. "Things is tough, for man and beast," he rambled on to himself. "Seems like all we do is do all we can to make it tougher. Lord, Lord!"

The children listened to everything he said. There were a bunch of them that day, even some who lived around the corner on Catalpa Street, like Perry and Archie. Word had spread that there was generally something interesting doing in Cockleburr Quarters. Whenever Jake Brown came in sight, the kids came running.

He was a renter now, not a squatter. He earned his rent by working at the Animal Hospital weekends and early in the morning. Usually he was back in the

Quarters by noon, and the kids were waiting for him to appoint the captains for the day. Each captain could choose a lieutenant to give orders to. Everybody had a turn to be boss.

There was a mess-picker-upper captain, a lime-layer captain, a can-squusher captain and a junk-sorter captain. There was a dog-feeder captain, a dog-brusher captain, a mange-goop-spreader captain and a dog-pan-washer captain. There was a water-pan-filler captain; Jake said he was the most important one of all. Jake was always thinking up jobs, and if he didn't think them up, they just happened, like this problem of catching the cats.

While they were waiting for the cats to go into the traps, Jake talked about defleaing cats. He said he would get some flea powder at the Animal Hospital. When cats were scared, like these, it was hard to put anything on them. Maybe the veterinarian would rub some on when he wormed them. If a cat was used to being handled, the best way to deflea him was to comb his coat with a fine-tooth comb. "Nobody figured that out, did they?" He chuckled. "So nobody gets the prize."

"Aw," muttered Bo. "That ain't fair. How we supposed to know that?"

"You supposed to make it your business to find out, that's how."

"Nuts."

By that time the mammy cat and her kittens had gone into the traps. They were so hungry they couldn't resist the smell of food. They crouched in the traps, their ragged fur sticking through the wire mesh. Their eyes were wide and glassy with fright.

Jake groaned, "Lord, Lord!"

"What's the matter, Jake?"

Jake pointed to the cats. "How many cats you see?"

The children giggled. Even the youngest one there could count to three.

"Come on," Jake urged them.

"Three."

"You know how many cats *I* see? I see a million."

"A million! Hoo, you kidding!" Bo said.

"No, I'll prove it to you. How many kittens did the mammy cat have last time?"

"Five; but something got 'em."

"Those yellow kittens, they from time before last," Sue Jean explained. "They was more of that batch, but they died, too."

"That's ten kittens, say, that mammy cat had last year. All right, when I look at her, I see all them kittens. And if we bring her back from the Animal Hospital and turn her a-loose, she'll have ten more."

Nobody said anything. What was there to say?

Jake repeated, "Ten kittens a year. She live five years, how many kittens is that?"

They counted. Hoo, man!

But Jake wasn't through. "Those two yellow kittens, they just about big enough to go into the kitten business themselves. They's both girls. Way I figure it, we soon have kittens running out of our ears."

Dolph knew all about the cost of dog and cat food, and how fast it went. "We ain't got that much money," he said. "We won't ever have enough money to feed all them cats."

Myrtis watched Jake uneasily. "You ain't going to kill them, are you, Jake?"

"Ought to."

Myrtis and Sue Jean and the other girls tuned up to cry. Lilboy squatted down close to the traps as if to guard them.

"There's another way, though," Jake said.

"Oh no!" Dolph flared. "I know about that. Carry them off in a sack, that's what they do. No way. You can't do that."

Jake shook his head. "No, dumping them ain't right. Killing ain't, either. Kill all the kittens in town, they's always more to come. But the veterinarian, he can fix these cats so they won't have any more kittens as long as they live. He'll operate on them, just like they do people in the hospital, and in a few days they'll be as good as new. Better. Because all them kittens won't never be born, and won't never go hungry."

"And they won't never get carried off in a sack!" cried Myrtis.

"And the food'll last a lot longer," Dolph said.

Jake took the cats to the Animal Hospital. Mr. Speck gave him a cut-rate taxi ride and let Dolph and Myrtis go along for free. They paid the veterinarian all the money they had left from the salvage business, and had to promise more.

142

When Mr. Speck took them back to the Quarters, he stopped and got out of his car to look around. "What's been going on?" he asked. "Some kind of a clean-up campaign?"

They explained about the worm war and the salvage business. "We just got that one pile of trash left," Bo said.

"We squushes the cans so dogs and cats can't get they snouts stuck in them," Marvin told him.

Myrtis added, "And all the broken glass we find, we put it in that box. So nobody cuts theyselves."

"Thing to do is get the trash hauled off, finish the job," Mr. Speck said. "I'll speak to the landlord myself and tell him how much better the place looks."

Emeline was watering the plants at the side of her house, and she heard that. "Don't you go tell him nothing," she called. "He's liable to raise the rent."

"But Emeline, it's no more than right. Nothing's been done to fix up the Quarters since I can remember."

"It's better that way," Emeline said stubbornly. "You stir up a landlord, it's like stirring up a pond, all the mud come to the top. Leave him alone, he'll leave us alone."

Mr. Speck shook his head. He knew he couldn't win an argument with Emeline Burch. He saw Tory and whistled. "Hmm-hmm! That dog's looking fat and sassy these days."

Tory sat at a safe distance from Emeline and watched what went on. Her one good eye was clear

143

and shining. Her coat was thick and smooth. The black part was blacker, the tan part shaded from pale cream to a bright copper color. There was a neat white patch on her muzzle and a line of white running up between her eyes to the top of her head. She had a white vest, three white socks, and white on the tip of her tail. Nobody had known there was any white on Tory until she dried out after her first dip. Before that she was just rusty black and dirty tan.

Tory seemed to know that she looked well. She seemed to smile, showing pink gums, and swept the ground with her tail.

"Mangy look better, too!" cried Lilboy.

"He does, for a fact," Mr. Speck agreed.

"We put mange goop on him every day," Lilboy bragged.

The hair was beginning to grow back over Mangy's bare patches, and the redness was going out of the sore places. "Lucky his mange is the kind we can cure," Jake said. "We keep the fleas and ticks off him, he going to be a new dog."

Mr. Speck had caught sight of Shaggy. "What kind of a dog is that?" When Jake had cut off all the tangles and mats in Shaggy's coat, there wasn't much dog left. Mr. Speck threw back his head and haw-hawed. "He looks to me like he went to sleep in the barber's chair."

XXIII

CHANGES

Dolph went every other day to water the yard for one of the Little Leaveners who was out of town. He had other regular customers, too. Sometimes he helped out at the Corner Store, and was paid in dog food. He kept his promise to give the money he made to Emeline. She always gave some back, although she had no use for Tory, much less for the stray dogs and cats Dolph was feeding.

When he wasn't working, there was always something interesting going on in Cockleburr Quarters. Mrs. Randall's Bible stories (with refreshments) were popular. So were Bo Slocum's arithmetic lessons—believe it or not.

Bo had kept on thinking about what Jake said about the cats and kittens. He undertook to figure out just how many kittens the mammy cat would have had if she had not been spayed. He wrote it down this way:

1st year:	Mammy cat has 10 kittens.		
	Mammy + 10 kits	=	11 cats.
2nd year:	Mammy cat has 10 kittens.		
	10 kits + 11 cats	=	21 cats.
	1st year kits have 10 kits each.		
	100 kits + 21 cats	=	121 cats.
3rd year:	Mammy cat has 10 kits.		
	10 kits + 121 cats	=	131 cats.
	1st year kits have 10 kits each.		
	100 kits + 131 cats	=	231 cats.
	2nd year kits have 10 kits each.		
	100 kits + 231 cats	=	331 cats.
4th year:	Mammy cat has 10 kits.		
	10 kits + 331 cats	=	341 cats.
	1st year kits have 10 kits each.		
	100 kits + 341 cats	=	441 cats.
	2nd year kits have 10 kits each.		
	100 kits + 441 cats	=	541 cats.
	3rd year kits have 10 kits each.		
	100 kits + 541 cats	=	641 cats.
5th year:	Mammy cat has 10 kits.		
	10 kits + 641 cats	=	651 cats.
	1st year kits have 10 kits each.		
	100 kits + 651 cats	=	751 cats.
	2nd year kits have 10 kits each.		
	100 kits + 751 cats	=	851 cats.
	3rd year kits have 10 kits each.		
	100 kits + 851 cats	=	951 cats.
	4th year kits have 10 kits each.		
	100 kits + 951 cats	=	1051 cats.

When he got that far, Bo began to be confused, but he wouldn't admit it. Instead, he showed the younger children how to add and subtract and divide, and they thought he knew everything. Marvin and Sue Jean stuck with the cat problem. They thought they could work it out with toothpicks. They ran out of toothpicks and used little sticks. Albert heard about it and offered to run off the figures on a calculating machine they had at the gas station. He used up several rolls of paper on the problem.

Dolph wasn't all that fond of arithmetic, but he liked the feeling that things were happening. He wished the summer would last forever. But that was impossible. School was due to start soon.

Clara took Dolph and Myrtis to town to buy new school clothes. That night when Pete came to see her, Clara had Myrtis dress up to show off her new things. Then she started on Dolph. "Come on," she coaxed, "put on your nice new clothes and show Pete how nice you can look."

"Not me," Dolph sulked. He was mad because he hadn't grown a bit since they bought his last year's clothes. He had worn them out; he hadn't outgrown them. He hated being so little and skinny. Wasn't he ever going to grow? Now Myrtis was nearly as tall as he was.

"Now, Dolph, be nice." Clara was ashamed of the way Dolph was acting before Pete.

"Let's go out on the porch," Pete said. He said it to Clara, but Dolph and Myrtis went along. They liked to listen in to grown-up talk sometimes; sometimes it was better than TV. Walter and Harrison had been put to bed. Some of the neighbors were sitting out in the Cotten's yard, visiting. Everybody could hear what everybody said.

They were all talking about the housing project behind the Quarters. It was finished at last, and people were moving out of the Quarters into the Project. Mr. Wheeler stopped on his way down the Alley to ask, "When you moving out, Miz Cotten?"

"We're all right here."

"Sure, but now that the Quarters is sold?"

"Sold?"

"Ain't you heard? The whole Quarters going to be cleared off to make room for more apartments."

"You sure?"

"Sure I'm sure. Ask the rent collector if you don't believe me."

Dolph didn't want to believe it. If the Quarters was torn down, Jake would have to move on, for sure. It couldn't happen. It mustn't happen. Just when things were going so good.

But the next afternoon when the rent collector came around, he said it was true that the Quarters was sold. Not only that, but the landlord sent word that everybody had to move out by the end of the month. After he left, the families in Cockleburr Quarters visited up and down the Alley talking over the news.

"Won't be no trouble to clear out the Quarters. Eat some onions, blow a strong breath, and the whole place'll collapse," Bo Slocum's sister said.

"We lucky to have the Project to move into," said

Mrs. Wheeler. "Everything nice and new. It's got its own Laundromat, and air conditioners all over."

"And low rent!"

"You watch and see; when they tear down the Quarters, all our rats and roaches'll move into the Project."

"We ain't had no rats since that yellow cat took up with us. We'll just take her with us when we move."

"I heard that the Project don't allow pets."

"I ain't talking about pets. I'd like to see anybody pet that yellow cat—you try, she take your hand off. But man, she's a mouser."

"It won't make no difference. No cats nor dogs allowed in the Project. I heard it straight."

That did it. Dolph felt the blow in his stomach. Even if Jake would move into the Project, which he wouldn't, there wouldn't be any place there for Tory. And what about the Burch family? Where were they going to go? It seemed as if the world were falling apart.

He looked around for Emeline. "She gone in the house," Myrtis told him. Dolph ran indoors to find her.

Emeline sat with her elbows on the kitchen table, her head in her hands. When Dolph burst in with his question, "We going to move into the Project?" she flared up as if she had just been waiting for someone to press her anger button. "Leave me alone!" Dolph waited stubbornly, while she looked over his head at the wall. After a long pause, she added, "Ain't no place for a garden in the Project. Just a big, paved patio in the middle."

Dolph let out a sigh of relief. No place for a garden. His mother would never live in a place like that. "Where we going to live?" He asked.

"You tell me."

"Well, they's lots of places."

"But not where the rent's as cheap as here. I been asking around. Rent's sky high."

Was Mamma actually thinking of moving into the Project, after all? If she did, there would never be a chance of changing her mind about keeping Tory. And what would happen to Mangy and Shaggy and the yellow cats when the Quarters was gone? The black mammy cat was taken care of—she had moved into Mrs. Randall's garage, and Mrs. Randall let her stay, because she was spayed.

"Run along," Emeline said. "No use to stick out your lip." She dropped her chin back into her hands.

A few days later there was more bad news. Mrs. Randall was taken to the hospital. She left word for Dolph to water her flower beds and her ferns, and to get food at the Corner Store for the mammy cat. It might be a while before she came home.

Dolph felt trouble piling up on him in a great big lump. They were going to have to move somewhere, and Tory and Shaggy and Mangy and the kittens had to go somewhere—and on top of all that, Jake was already talking about moving on. It was high time,

150

he said. What was the use of waiting until they tore down the house on top of his head?

Dolph couldn't see anything but trouble ahead. To keep from thinking about it, he worked hard, trying to earn all he could before school started. He had Mrs. Randall's chores to do while she was in the hospital, and he made the rounds of the Little Leaveners every day. But he couldn't really get the trouble out of his mind. Emeline was in a bad mood nearly all the time. Albert worked late to stay out of her way. And every time Dolph saw Clara and Pete they were whispering. Only Harrison and Walter were not gloomy.

One day an errand took Dolph near Winnie Street. He wondered about the puppies, Lep and Dice and Bubba. He wondered how they were. Would they know him? Had they grown much? Were they fat and sassy? Suddenly in a big hurry, he found the way to where Joyce lived.

Joyce came to the door holding a transistor at her ear, shuffling her feet to loud music. Dolph yelled to make himself heard. "Where's the puppies?"

"The what?"

"The puppies. You know, I'm the one give you and another girl those puppies a while ago."

"Oh. You're whatsisname. I remember you." She jerked her head and shuffled her feet and swiveled her hips.

"Dolph. I'm Dolph. Where's the puppies?"

"Oh, puppies," Joyce said. "I don't have mine any

151

more. My daddy, he said if I'd get rid of the puppy he'd buy me the transistor. So I give it away."

"Give him away? Dice? But you said you *wanted* him. I didn't say you could give him away!"

"He messed in the house and cried all night." Shuffle, shuffle, jerk, jerk.

"He didn't know better. He was just a pup, never been away from his mammy." Dolph's face was screwed up with anger and pity.

Joyce made a face to match. "Boo-hoo!" She mocked. "Boo-hoo!"

Dolph wanted to hit her but he didn't. "That other girl I give the puppy to," he said, "where does she live?"

Joyce shuffled and jerked in a circle. "Betty. Third house down, on the left. Yeah, yeah. Third, third, third. Left, left, left. Yeah, yeah, yeah." Dolph walked off, fuming. She called after him, "Betty's brother run over her pup in the driveway. It was dark, he didn't know it was there."

Dolph felt weak with misery. Tears welled up inside him. Joyce stopped shuffling and lowered the volume on the radio. "Betty cried like everything. She really did."

"Boo-hoo!" Dolph yelled at her. "Boo-hoo!" It was better to yell than to cry in front of Joyce. He ran off furiously. As soon as he was out of sight he stopped to get his breath. He couldn't outrun his misery.

On the way home he had to pass the house on Julia Street where he and Myrtis had left Bubba. The same

152

woman was standing in her doorway, with the little boy on her hip. She saw Dolph and called out, "Hey!"

Dolph stopped. He didn't see Bubba.

"Ain't you the boy give us the puppy dog? I was wishing you'd come back." The woman came outside. "Have you got any more left?"

Dolph shook his head.

"I'd gladly take another, if you did. Tracy didn't ever have anything to play with he liked as much as that pup."

Dolph said nothing, thinking of Bubba with his floppy ears and his paunch like a football.

"Tracy played with that puppy all day long. It was a circus to see them. Then one night the pup acted sick, and the next morning he was dead. I don't know what ailed him." She smiled brightly. "Ain't you got another?"

"No," Dolph muttered, "I ain't got no more." No more for such as you, he thought, walking away, head down.

Dolph made his way through the woods on top of Cockleburr Hill and down to the place where the shack had been. He had not been there since the fire. He felt bruised and sore inside when he thought of Bubba and Dice and Lep, but he couldn't help thinking about them. And the others: Lassie who was run over the night of the fire, and Coonhound and Tansy, who ran away and hid with Tory. And Blackie and Whitey who died first. Eight puppies, all gone. Tory tried so hard to raise them, and he had tried so hard

to help her—and they had both failed. It seemed as if there wasn't much of a place for puppies in this world.

From where Dolph stood he could look down on the whole neighborhood: Short Cockleburr Street, the Corner Store, the shabby old Quarters, with the church in front and the big brick housing project behind. It was late afternoon. Over the hills across town the red, red sun was setting. A smoky haze hung over the houses and trees below.

He was looking down on a big bowl, he thought, and in the bowl was the great lump of dough Mrs. Randall had told him about—the world and all the people in it. A great, gray, heavy, tasteless, useless lump. Too heavy to lift, too thick to get through, too big to get away from.

As he had done once before, after the white puppy's funeral, Dolph laid himself down on the hillside and cried until he couldn't cry any more. The world is a lump, all right, thought Dolph. Big enough and heavy enough to weigh me down forever. Make it lighter? Make it rise? No way. No way.

XXIV

SPROUTS

The Wheelers and the Slocums moved out of Cockleburr Quarters and into the Project. Mangy and Shaggy were left behind. Because of the high board fence between, people in the Project had to walk clear around the block to visit the Quarters, so they didn't very often. Lilboy did come back twice to put mange goop on Mangy, but after that he forgot.

Mangy and Shaggy moved in with Jake. But what good would that do? In a couple of weeks everyone would have gone. Every day Jake said he was moving on.

Dolph felt worse and worse as more and more houses became empty. His lump of misery and fear grew. Emeline didn't say she was going to move into the Project, but she didn't say she wasn't, either. She couldn't find anywhere else that suited her. Mrs. Randall was still in the hospital, and Mrs. Whitaker told Dolph she didn't think she was doing so well. Worst of all was the fear of losing Jake.

I wisht Jake had never come to the Quarters at all, Dolph thought. He pushed into the back of his mind an idea he had to help Tory. It was really just the seed of an idea that had come too late to sprout. Dolph buried it under his misery. What was the use? Every day might be the last one he'd see Jake. What was the use of anything?

Tory seemed to feel that something was wrong. She stuck close to Dolph, wouldn't let him out of her sight. And Dolph stuck as close as he could to Jake.

One evening Dolph was moping nearby while Jake worked in Emeline's garden. Tory lay just around the corner of the house, close enough to see them, but far enough away to make a quick getaway if Emeline came out. Jake was digging little ditches to carry water down the rows of tomatoes and corn. It was wonderful how neatly and quickly Jake handled a hoe: chop, chop, chop.

"Wake up, Boy," he called to Dolph. "Turn on the water when I say."

Dolph sulked, not moving from where he leaned against a clothesline post.

"Hey, Dolph!"

"What?"

"Turn it on."

"Aw, nuts," said Dolph. "It's just plain silly to sweat in a garden that's gone be bulldozed flat before long."

Jake looked at him, then back at his work. "Guess it is pretty silly, at that," he agreed.

"Then why don't you quit it?"

Chop, chop, chop. "Well, the corn don't know

157

enough to quit it," Jake said. "And long as green things keep sprouting, seems a shame not to help 'em sprout." He laid the hose in the ditch. "Turn on the water."

Dolph walked slowly to the hydrant and turned it on. He could feel the water coursing through the hose. He went over to watch it gush out and trickle down the furrow Jake had deepened, sinking rapidly into the thirsty ground. The smell of green leaves, limp after the long, hot day, mingled with the smell of damp earth. Overhead the chimney swifts twittered in the evening sky. Mosquitoes hummed.

As Dolph watched, he seemed to see the stems of the plants stand straighter, the leaves fatten and freshen with the moisture. The idea he had buried in his mind stirred. "Jake?"

"Hunh?" Jake leaned on his hoe and looked down at Dolph, his mournful cheeks hanging in folds.

"Can the veterinarian operate on Tory, like he did on the cats?"

"You mean spay her, so she won't have puppies?" Dolph nodded.

"Sure he can."

"Will you take her to the Animal Hospital and have her fixed, Jake?"

Jake sighed. "You're talking about money, Boy."

"I know it," Dolph said, "but I'll pay something every week. The veterinarian will do it that way if you ast him to."

Jake hunched his shoulders. "Now look," he said, "You're talking about spending money on a dog you can't keep."

158

"I am so going to keep Tory!" Dolph cried desperately.

"Hah!" Jake went back to his work. "You try to keep her in the Project—" chop, chop, "they'll call the Law and put her in the pound." Chop, chop. "Then they shoot her." Chop, chop. "That's the way it is, Boy. You might as well give up."

Dusk was falling, heavy and hot. They slapped at the mosquitoes nipping their damp skin. Dolph turned away, drooping. Hoo, man! he thought, I'm going to walk right out of here. I'll walk away and keep moving on, like Jake. That would be the life.

Jake pushed some dirt with his foot to mend his ditch where the water was escaping. "Well, I reckon we can manage to get Tory spayed," he said after a long silence, "Once she's spayed, we might find somebody would take her."

Giving Tory away wasn't what Dolph had in mind. After what happened to the puppies, he thought, maybe it wasn't any better than shooting her. But at least he could fix it so she wouldn't have to have any more hungry puppies to raise, puppies nobody really wanted.

When the water had run long enough, Jake took the hose and sluiced himself down. He used his shirt for a towel before putting it on. He told Dolph, "Go tell your mamma I'm ready to go." That was his way of asking for the greens and cornbread Emeline kept for him on the stove.

XXV

GHOST TOWN

Jake took Tory to the Animal Hospital one day and brought her back the next, with three neat stitches down the middle of her stomach. She felt fine; so fine and frisky, in fact, that Jake kept her in the house for a few days to keep her from running around. At the end of the week, Jake took her back to the hospital to have her stitches removed.

Jake asked at the Animal Hospital, at Albert's gas station, and everywhere he went, if anybody wanted a cat or a dog. Nobody wanted Tory, not after they heard that she was half-blind and crippled. He found a place for one of the yellow cats at a store where a mouser was needed, and he found a man who wanted a couple of dogs for his farm. The man arranged to come by and get Mangy and Shaggy.

Time was running out. Jake and the Burches and the Cottens were the only renters left in the Quarters. It was like a ghost town with all the empty houses.

160

Every night Dolph went to sleep wondering whether Jake would still be there next day, and whether Emeline would find somewhere they could move besides the Project. He lay awake a long time, slapping mosquitoes and smelling the sweetness of Emeline's four-o'clocks.

The Cottens moved out. Marvin's and Sue Jean's uncle came to haul off their furniture in a pickup, and their aunt came in a car for the family. They took the other yellow cat with them. They were going to live with relatives in the country. After they all drove away, the quiet in the Quarters was something else.

When Jake came home from work that morning, there were only two children, Dolph and Myrtis, to meet him. It was a mournful meeting. Only the dogs were happy. They didn't know this was the day the man was coming to take Shaggy and Mangy away.

Dolph and Myrtis sat with Jake on his porch and helped brush Shaggy's funny-looking coat. They searched all the dogs for fleas. Mangy's hair hadn't really grown back, but his sore places had healed and he didn't need mange goop any more.

A car rattled to a stop and honked. Jake went to meet the big, red-faced man with baggy pants who got out. The man looked at Mangy and Shaggy. "I thought you said they was good looking dogs," he said.

"I told you they would be good looking when they coats come in new," Jake answered.

"Well, I don't care how ugly they are, if they kill armadillos," the man said.

161

"You'll have to train them to."

The man snorted. "A dog's an armadillo dog or he ain't. I got no use for a dog won't kill varmints. Come on; let's load them in." The man made a move toward Mangy, who backed off and watched him suspiciously. It hadn't been long since he and Shaggy had known nothing but yells and kicks. He recognized the signs.

"Wait a minute, Mister," Jake said. "You just hold the car door open. "I'll get a rope on the dogs and put them in for you."

"That dog looks mean to me."

Jake got a rope and talked quietly to Mangy and Shaggy. The man opened the trunk of his car.

"You don't aim to carry the dogs in the trunk, do you?" Jake spoke politely, as if he were making conversation, while he reached down to rub Mangy's ears.

"Where else?" The man waited by the open trunk. "You don't expect me to carry a couple of dirty dogs inside my car."

Dolph and Myrtis thought that Mangy and Shaggy were cleaner than that car. They hoped Jake would tell the man so. He didn't, but they could see that he was slipping the rope off over Mangy's head while he pretended to rub his ears. He gave a quick little shove at Mangy with his knee, acting all the time as if he were trying to catch him again. Mangy scooted under the porch and Shaggy followed.

"Watch out!" yelled the man. "Now you gone and let him get away."

"Goshsake!" Jake acted surprised.

163

The man's face was purple. "Well, catch him, can't you? I can't wait all day."

"Too bad you had your trip for nothing," Jake said. "I ain't going to put no dogs in no trunk. With the sun beating down, it's the same thing as putting biscuits in the oven."

"I always leave a crack for air," the man argued.

"If they don't cook, the exhaust fumes make them sick," Jake said. "I'm sorry for your trouble, Mister, but I won't put dogs in that thing."

"Now look here. You gave them to me. It was a deal."

"I ain't gone back on the deal. You can have them if you can catch them."

The man took a step toward the porch. The dogs drew further back underneath, showing their teeth and the whites of their eyes. The man gave up the idea. He knew he would look silly if he got down on his hands and knees and tried to grab those dogs. Dolph and Myrtis were wishing he'd try it.

The man drove away. Jake sat down on the steps and laughed. He laughed so hard tears squeezed out of his eyes. Myrtis and Dolph sat beside him and laughed, too. They were glad of an excuse to let themselves go, break up the sad silence. Mangy, Shaggy and Tory came frolicking up to them, waving their tails. The mammy cat sat on Mrs. Randall's fence and washed her face.

When the children had their laugh out, Jake's shoulders were still shaking. They realized suddenly that he was crying, not laughing any more. His tears were real tears. He burst out, hoarsely, "I'd druther shoot them dogs than to let them be abused. If it comes to that, I will."

Dolph and Myrtis sat, stunned.

Jake went on, half to them, half to himself, "Lord, Lord!" He wiped his face on his sleeve. "It's an awful thing to let someone trust you. Once you do, you're stuck." He rubbed Tory's ears, then pushed her away. "Stuck."

Stuck! Dolph thought. Stuck in the lump. Lord, Lord!

Jake turned his face away from them. "Git on home, kids," he said.

Seeing a grown man cry was too much for Dolph and Myrtis. Grown people weren't supposed to cry. Dolph grabbed Myrtis by the arm and ran home.

XXVI

TOMATOES

Emeline came home later that evening, fuming. She had been looking at places to rent. There was something wrong with all of them. "You never heard of such prices," she said the minute she walked in the kitchen, where Albert and Dolph and Myrtis were having a snack. "Landlords ast you for a leg and an arm."

"They's bound to be places we can afford, Mamma," Albert said. "I'll be paying for my keep, working at the filling station after school. Clara pays her way. Even Dolph earns. No freeloaders in the family now." Emeline frowned, but Albert knew better than to mention Janetta or Uncle Leon in front of her. She never called their names, but if anybody asked her about them, she looked the questioner in the eye and said, "They gone for good."

Albert hurried on, "With the money James sends home, we're rich compared to some."

"Sure we're rich," Emeline agreed sarcastically. "But the rent ain't all. Mr. Casper, he offered me a

166

nice house right back of theirs, low rent and room for a garden, too, but—"

"See!"

"I see I'd be living under my boss's eye; beck and call, day and night. No thanks. Miz Casper's worse than them social workers; we wouldn't have a moment's peace, couldn't call my soul my own. Besides, she'd be wanting me to come cook for company every night if I lived close by. Why you think I've lived across town from them all these years?"

"O.K., O.K. What about this side of town? Mr. Holly, right down there on Short Cockleburr Street, next to James's lot, he got a rent house in his back yard, and I know it's vacant, because the folks lived there moved into the Project."

"I already seen Mr. Holly," Emeline snapped. "He won't rent to us, says they's too many of us, with the babies and all. His rent is high, but I'd a paid it somehow if I had to. I was thinking I could make a garden on James's lot, live next door, it would be kind of nice," she sighed.

Dolph pricked up his ears. A garden on James's lot . . . James's lot! It came over him in a flash: he could have a dog house there, a place for Tory to live, right next door to him. James wouldn't mind—and James was the one to say, not Emeline. "Mamma!" Dolph cried.

"Mr. Holly won't rent to us, I said!"

"Oh, Mamma, ast him again!" Myrtis begged.

"I ast him. I ast him. He's made up his mind. He says there's a young couple, 'thout children, looking at

167

the house. He's going to give it to them if they decide. It's Mr. Holly's house; he got a right to choose."

She went on telling all the things that were wrong with the other places she'd seen. Albert quit listening and turned on the TV in the front room. Dolph and Myrtis stayed in the kitchen with Emeline.

"Mamma," Myrtis piped up after a long silence, "When I'm grown up I'm going to make a million dollars and I'll give it all to you."

Emeline pulled the little girl's head against her and squeezed her quickly. "You do that."

"How do you make a million dollars?" Myrtis asked. Emeline laughed right out. "Don't ast me," she said. "But I can tell you how not to. Quit school and start having babies, like I did, like Clara and—like we did. That's how not to."

"Now Albert's changed his mind and going back to school, will he make a million dollars?"

"Maybe." Emeline pushed her chair back from the table. Dolph and Myrtis watched her. Dolph was too miserable even to make fun of Myrtis and her million dollars. "Now don't you two just hang around looking downhearted," Emeline said, "Make yourselves useful. Take that pan and pick the tomatoes, all that are ripe. Some snap beans, too."

Dolph and Myrtis went out. They were glad to have something to do. They liked the warm, damp feel of the loose dirt under their bare feet, and the strong, pungent smell the tomato plants gave off. Tory lay a little way off, waiting for them.

168

Cockleburr Quarters was quiet, almost empty. Sounds came over the Project fence: doors slamming, children playing, a radio blaring.

Dolph and Myrtis carried their harvest into the kitchen. Emeline was trimming Albert's hair. The TV was still going strong all by itself in the front room. They heard Clara come in, bringing Walter and Harrison from the Day-Care Center. She called, "Mamma?" Something in her voice made them all sit up and take notice.

Clara came into the kitchen like a breath of cool, fresh air, smiling. Albert took Walter, tossing him up to make him scream. Myrtis took Harrison in her lap. "Mamma," Clara announced, "I got something to tell you."

Dolph and Myrtis listened, all ears.

"Pete and I are going to get married! Mamma, we got it all set. He's going to that job in Houston and it starts next week. And, Mamma, Pete says we ought to take Harrison with us. Harrison and Walter just like brothers, it'd be a pity to part them. Pete's a good man, Mamma." Her eyes shone.

Emeline's eyes filled. Harrison squealed; Myrtis was jigging with excitement. Visions of weddings she had seen in pictures floated through her head. "Can I be in the wedding? Clara, can I?" Myrtis asked it over and over until Clara listened.

"Sure you can, Baby," Clara said. "You can dress up real nice. You can all be in it."

"Not me!" said Dolph.

169

"Not me!" said Albert. Dolph went over and stood beside him. "Not me! Not me!" Harrison babbled, echoed by Walter, "Nommee! Nommee!" And everyone started talking at the same time.

All at once Dolph had one of those bright ideas that Mrs. Randall said he was full of. He was sure this really was a bright one. "Hey, Mamma!" he cried. "Four isn't many. Four isn't a big family. Mamma, go tell Mr. Holly."

Nobody heard him but Albert. Albert spoke up. "That's right, Mamma. Clara and the babies gone, only you and me and Dolph and Myrtis. It wouldn't hurt to ast."

They explained to Clara about Mr. Holly's house. She smiled. "That's a nice place Mr. Holly got. I'd feel happy to know y'all was living there."

Emeline smoothed her dress and dabbed at her eyes. "I'll go see," she said. "Myrtis, you clean up the babies. Clara, you fix supper, and make Dolph help. Albert, you come with me."

Supper was ready and the babies were clean. Dolph and Myrtis couldn't wait for Emeline to come back. "Reckon what they talking about to take this long?" Dolph fretted.

"I could leave Mamma and be happy if I just knew she had somewhere nice to live," Clara murmured. She put the tomatoes in a big bowl in the middle of the table, where they glowed under the light. Dolph stared at them, thinking how good they were going to taste with pepper and salt. Suddenly

170

he grabbed the bowl off the table and made for the door.

"Where you going?" Myrtis cried, but he was gone.

Emeline and Albert were saying goodbye to Mr. and Mrs. Holly in their front yard when Dolph panted up. They all looked tired and stubborn; they had said all they had to say. Mr. Holly and his wife would have been willing to rent their house to the Burches, now that the family was smaller, but they would rather not have children making a racket, and they had halfway promised it to the other folks. . .

Dolph ran into the midst of them with the bowl of tomatoes. He held up the big, ripe, red globes. Mr. and Mrs. Holly each reached out and took one.

"Mamma raised 'em," Dolph said. "You can have 'em."

Emeline gave Dolph one of her looks, but Dolph kept his eyes on the tomatoes.

"Mmm, mmm!" said Mrs. Holly. She turned the tomato in her hands, put it to her nose and smelled it.

Mr. Holly said, "I ain't seen such tomatoes since I made a garden myself. Many a year ago. Before I got the high blood and had to give up any kind of work."

"Mamma raised 'em," Dolph repeated. "In that little old patch at the Quarters. She said, if she move into your place, she going to make a big garden, right next door to you, on James's lot."

The Hollys turned to look at the vacant lot, as if they had never seen it before. "That's James's lot?"

"Sure is," Dolph said, "and Mamma could make a

171

big garden there. I'd help her." He stepped back on Albert's foot. "Albert, too."

"Oh. Yeah. Yessir," said Albert, grinning at Dolph. "If we lived here, we'd raise corn and peas and beans and onions and squash and collards and tomatoes and —why, that lot, it's big enough to plant watermelons on."

"It is," Mr. Holly nodded. "It is for a fact. Plenty of sunshine, and the ground drains nice." The Hollys looked at each other. Mr. Holly took the bowl of tomatoes from Dolph and put it in Mrs. Holly's hands.

Emeline broke in, "We'd expect to sell most of our garden stuff, of course, Mr. Holly. The Corner Store will take all I can spare, and Dolph can sell all he can peddle with his wagon. But if we could come to an understanding about the rent, my garden could supply your table, easy, most of the year."

Dolph was always being surprised by grown people. Even your own mother, he thought; you never know for sure what goes on in her head. Listen to Emeline smooth-talking Mr. Holly into lowering the rent! He and Albert had to back off into the shadows to hide their grinning faces. Tory was crouched there behind the hedge, waiting. When they heard Emeline say, "That's right, then; we'll move in after the wedding," the boys and Tory raced toward home, leaving Emeline to follow them unhurriedly down Short Cockleburr Street.

172

XXVII

THE END?

After supper, Myrtis and Dolph and Tory went to tell Jake the news. He was sitting on his front steps with Shaggy and Mangy, looking at the big, full moon hanging over Cockleburr Hill.

Was it Jake? When they saw his face in the moonlight, they wondered. The deep, mournful wrinkles were there, just as deep and mournful as usual, but somehow he had a peaceful look.

Dolph began at once, "Jake, will you help me build a doghouse for Tory? Right away? Tomorrow? Will you?" Then he and Myrtis between them told Jake the good news about moving to Short Cockleburr Street where Emeline could have her garden and Dolph could keep Tory next door.

"Gawshsake!" Jake smiled. "Well, Dolph, look like you and Tory has landed on your feet."

Myrtis and Dolph jigged up and down and giggled. But soon they remembered. Cockleburr Quarters was coming down, Jake was moving on, and Mangy and Shaggy had nowhere to go.

Myrtis sat close to Jake on one side and Dolph sat on the other. It was very quiet. Dolph said in a small, shaky voice, "Jake—"

"Hunh?"

"Jake, when you going away?"

"I ain't in no hurry."

"You ain't?" Myrtis gaped at him in surprise.

"Jake! You going to stay?" Dolph nearly fell off the porch.

"I didn't say that."

"What you going to do, Jake?" Myrtis begged.

"Well, the veterinarian wants me to sleep nights at the Animal Hospital, keep an eye on the place for him."

"Can you take Mangy and Shaggy with you?"

"No, but what I'm thinking is, Miz Randall needs somebody to watch her place while she's in the hospital. I can do that, daytimes, and Mangy and Shaggy will make good watch dogs nights."

Myrtis cried, "Sure they will!"

Dolph was doubtful. "Did Miz Randall say you could?"

"No," Jake said, "But she ain't here to say I can't, neither."

They laughed together. The dogs felt the change in their feelings and began to leap and bark and run around in circles. Dolph seized one of Jake's hands and Myrtis the other. They pulled him to his feet.

"Come on," cried Dolph. "Come on, Jake! Let's go look where Tory's house is going to be."

They led Jake and the dogs down Cockleburr Street and across Catalpa and down Short Cockleburr to James's lot. It looked beautiful in the moonlight, they thought. Dolph and Myrtis ran here and there, arguing about where the garden would be and where to put Tory's house.

The dogs explored the lot in their own way, sniffing and pawing among the weeds. The place that interested them most was the old junked car. Shaggy and Mangy poked their noses inside and wagged their tails. Tory barked and barked. Dolph grinned. "Maybe Tory wants to live there."

"More likely some kind of a varmint in there."

They went and peered cautiously into the shell of the wrecked car. The shadows inside seemed to move; and then, in a patch of moonlight nearly as bright as daylight, they saw a small dog huddled on the torn upholstery, nursing a litter of newborn puppies. She looked up at them with the moon reflected in her eyes, and doubtfully moved her tail.

Note to the Reader:

The Kindness Club is an international club for boys and girls who want to help animals in need. Their pledge is: I PROMISE TO BE KIND TO ANIMALS AS WELL AS PEOPLE, AND TO SPEAK AND ACT IN DEFENSE OF ALL HELPLESS LIVING CREATURES.

To find out more about the Kindness Club, write:

THE KINDNESS CLUB
National Humane Education Center
Waterford, Virginia 22190